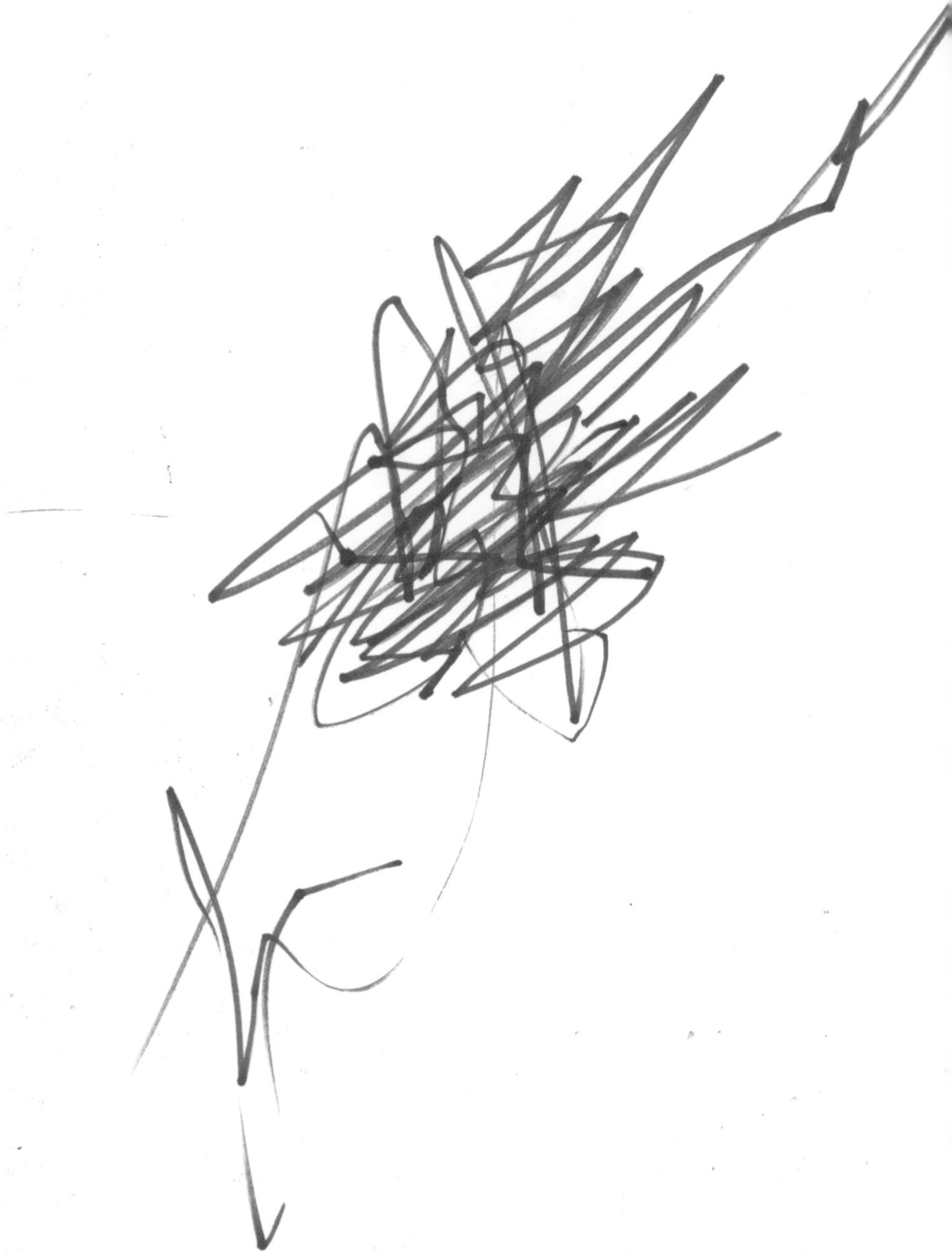

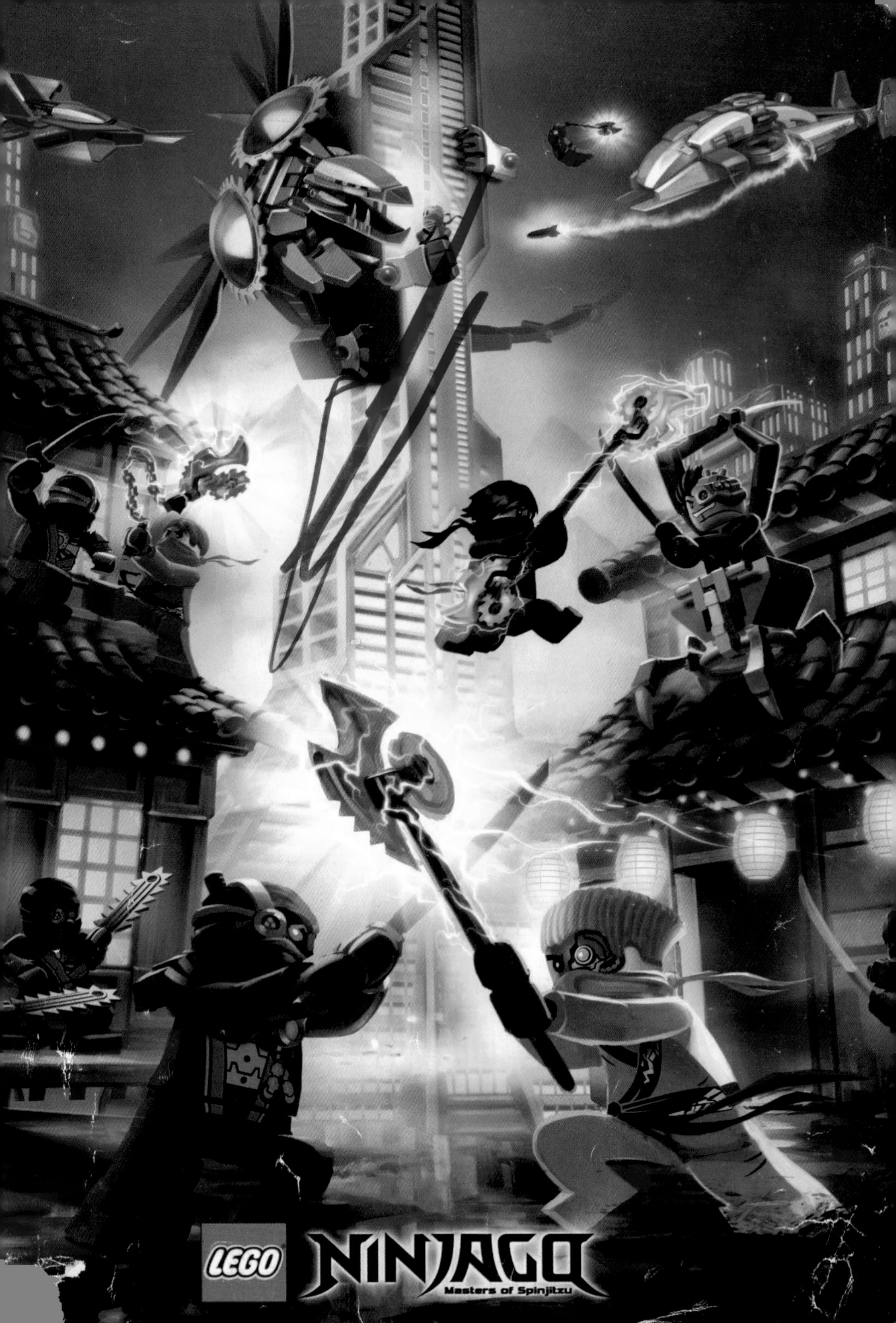
LEGO
NINJAGO
Masters of Spinjitzu

PAPERCUTZ™

LEGO® GRAPHIC NOVELS AVAILABLE FROM PAPERCUTZ

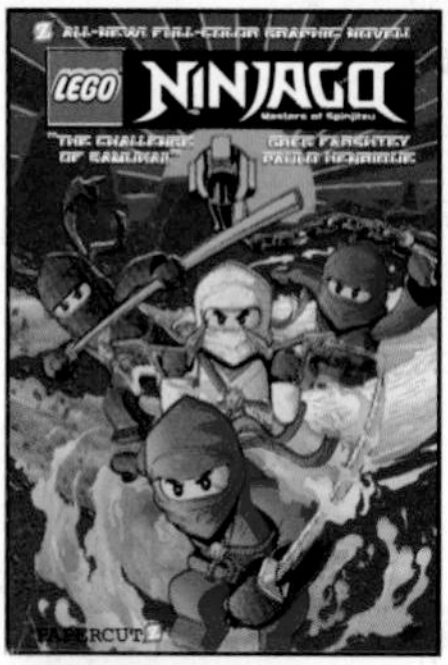
ALL-NEW! FULL-COLOR GRAPHIC NOVEL!
LEGO NINJAGO
"THE CHALLENGE OF SAMUKAI"
PAPERCUTZ
LEGO NINJAGO #1

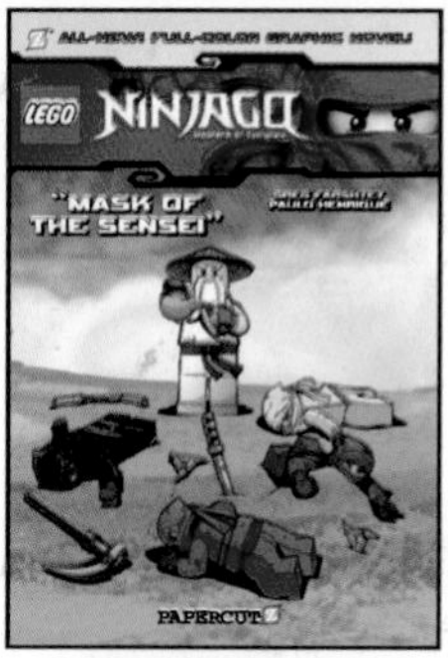
ALL-NEW! FULL-COLOR GRAPHIC NOVEL!
LEGO NINJAGO
"MASK OF THE SENSEI"
PAPERCUTZ
LEGO NINJAGO #2

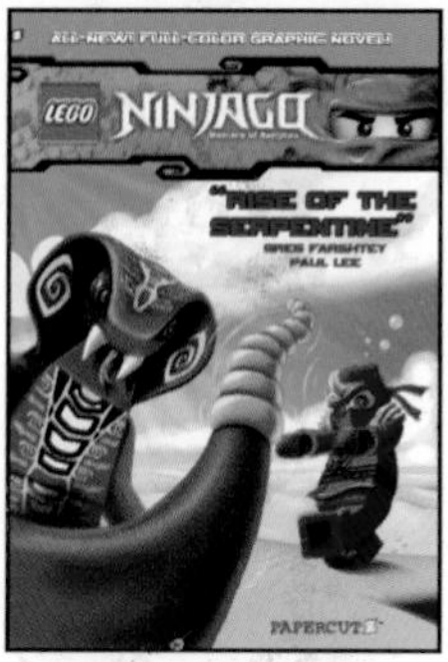
ALL-NEW! FULL-COLOR GRAPHIC NOVEL!
LEGO NINJAGO
"RISE OF THE SERPENTINE"
GREG FARSHTEY
PAUL LEE
PAPERCUTZ
LEGO NINJAGO #3

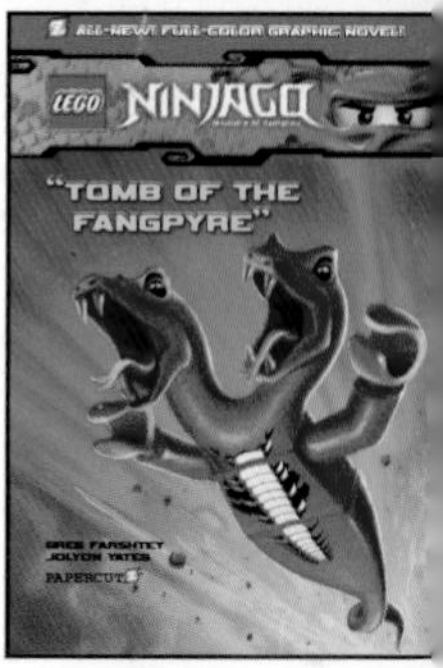
ALL-NEW! FULL-COLOR GRAPHIC NOVEL!
LEGO NINJAGO
"TOMB OF THE FANGPYRE"
GREG FARSHTEY
JOLYON YATES
PAPERCUTZ
LEGO NINJAGO #4

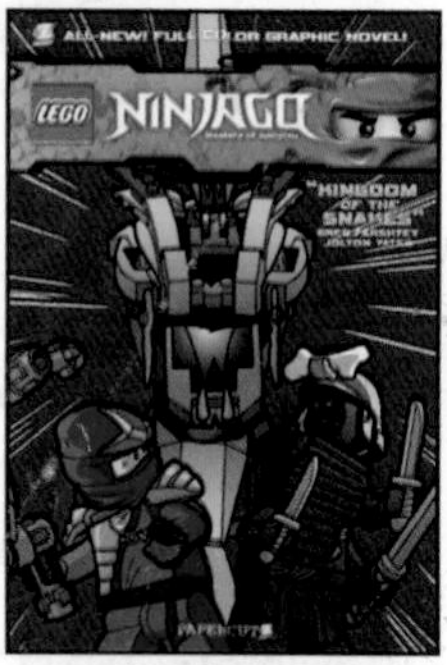
ALL-NEW! FULL-COLOR GRAPHIC NOVEL!
LEGO NINJAGO
"KINGDOM OF THE SNAKES"
GREG FARSHTEY
JOLYON YATES
PAPERCUTZ
LEGO NINJAGO #5

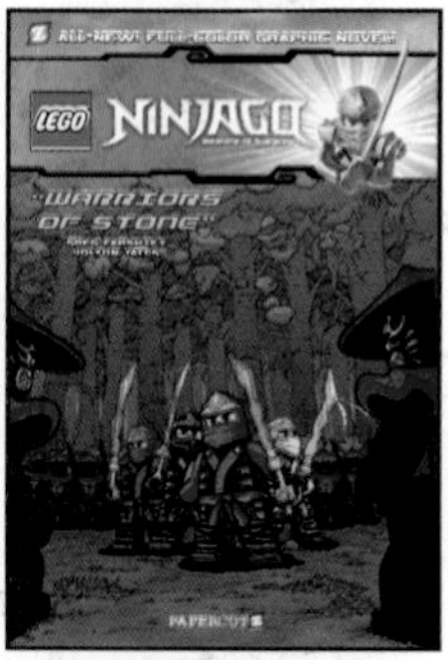
ALL-NEW! FULL-COLOR GRAPHIC NOVEL!
LEGO NINJAGO
"WARRIORS OF STONE"
PAPERCUTZ
LEGO NINJAGO #6

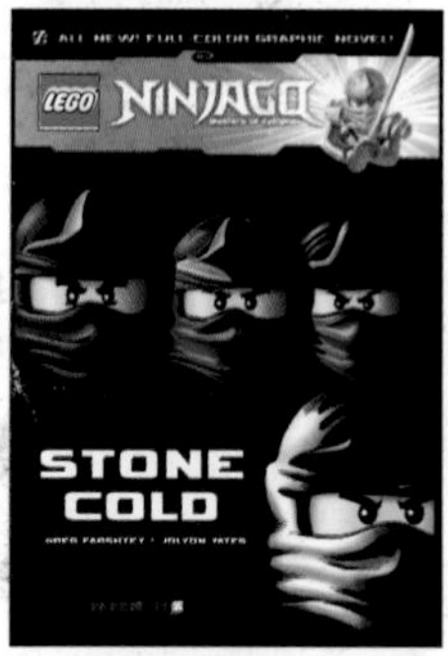
ALL NEW! FULL COLOR GRAPHIC NOVEL!
LEGO NINJAGO
STONE COLD
GREG FARSHTEY • JOLYON YATES
LEGO NINJAGO #7

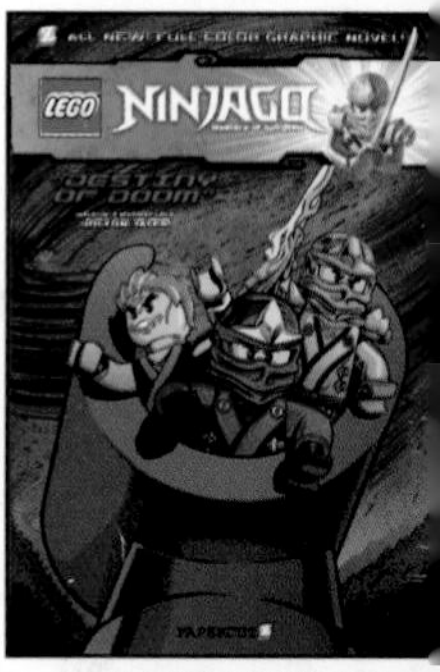
ALL-NEW! FULL-COLOR GRAPHIC NOVEL!
LEGO NINJAGO
"DESTINY OF DOOM"
PAPERCUTZ
LEGO NINJAGO #8

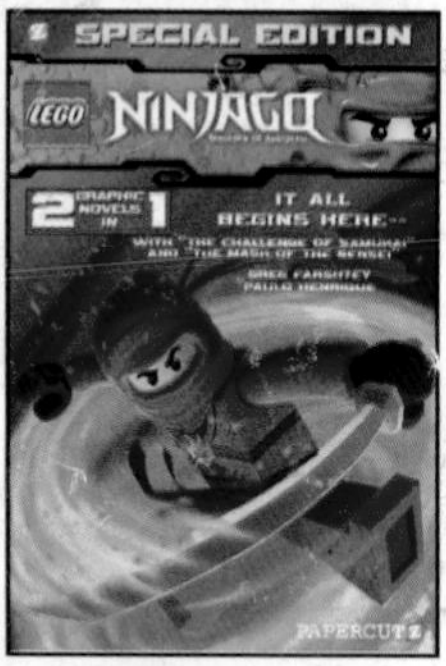
SPECIAL EDITION
LEGO NINJAGO
2 GRAPHIC NOVELS IN 1
IT ALL BEGINS HERE--
WITH "THE CHALLENGE OF SAMUKAI" AND "THE MASK OF THE SENSEI"
GREG FARSHTEY
PAULO HENRIQUE
PAPERCUTZ
SPECIAL EDITION #1
(Features stories from NINJAGO #1 & #2.)

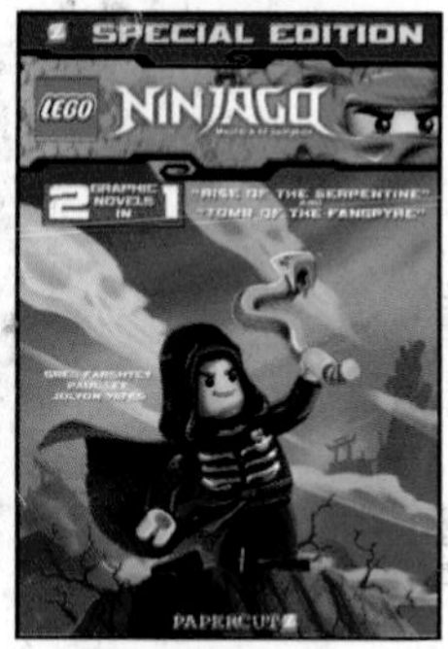
SPECIAL EDITION
LEGO NINJAGO
2 GRAPHIC NOVELS IN 1
"RISE OF THE SERPENTINE"
"TOMB OF THE FANGPYRE"
PAPERCUTZ
SPECIAL EDITION #2
(Features stories from NINJAGO #3 & #4.)

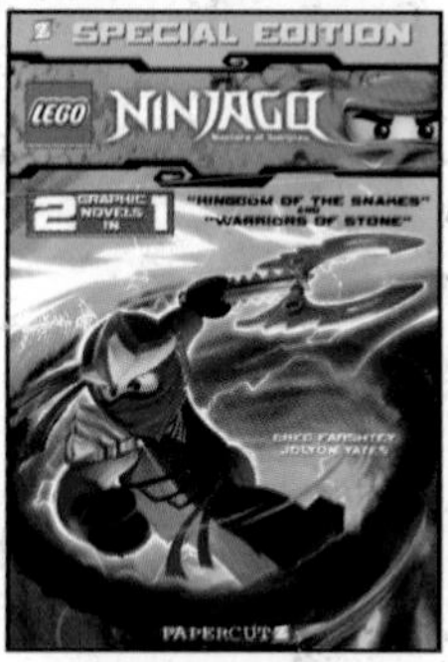
SPECIAL EDITION
LEGO NINJAGO
2 GRAPHIC NOVELS IN 1
"KINGDOM OF THE SNAKES"
"WARRIORS OF STONE"
GREG FARSHTEY
JOLYON YATES
PAPERCUTZ
SPECIAL EDITION #3
(Features stories from NINJAGO #5 & #6.)

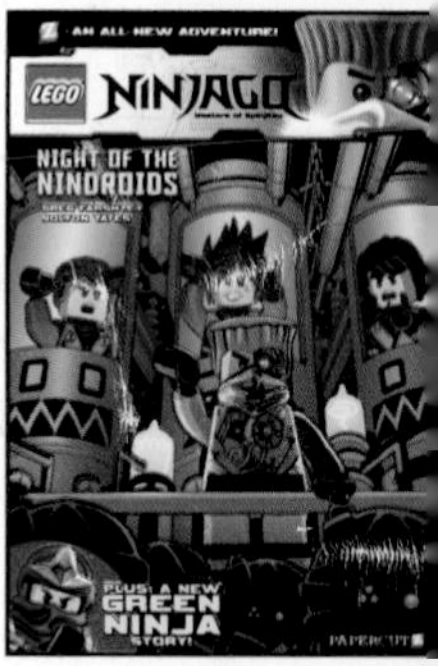
AN ALL NEW ADVENTURE!
LEGO NINJAGO
NIGHT OF THE NINDROIDS
GREG FARSHTEY
JOLYON YATES
PLUS A NEW GREEN NINJA STORY!
PAPERCUTZ
LEGO NINJAGO #9

COMING SOON!

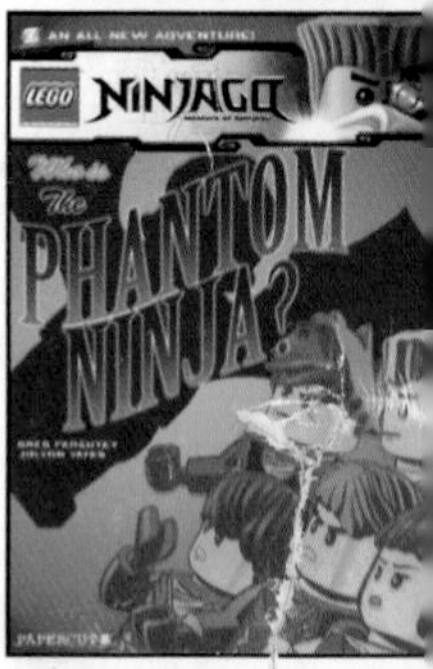
AN ALL NEW ADVENTURE!
LEGO NINJAGO
Who is The PHANTOM NINJA?
PAPERCUTZ
LEGO NINJAGO #10

LEGO® NINJAGO graphic novels are available in paperback and hardcover at booksellers everywhere.

LEGO® NINJAGO #1-10 are $6.99 in paperback, and $10.99 in hardcover. LEGO NINJAGO SPECIAL EDITION #1-3 are $10.99 in paperback only. You can also order online at papercutz.com. Or call 1-800-886-1223, Monday through Friday, 9 – 5 EST. MC, Visa, and AmEx accepted. To order by mail, please add $4.00 for postage and handling for first book ordered, $1.00 for each additional book and make check payable to NBM Publishing. Send to: Papercutz, 160 Broadway, Suite 700, East Wing, New York, NY 10038.

LEGO NINJAGO graphic novels are also available digitally wherever e-books are sold.

NIGHT OF THE NINDROIDS

Greg Farshtey – Writer

Jolyon Yates – Artist

Laurie E. Smith – Colorist

New York

LEGO® NINJAGO Masters of Spinjitzu
#9 "Night of the Nindroids"
Greg Farshtey – Writer
Jolyon Yates – Artist
Laurie E. Smith – Colorist
Bryan Senka – Letterer
Dawn K. Guzzo – Production
Beth Scorzato – Production Coordinator
Michael Petranek – Associate Editor
Jim Salicrup
Editor-in-Chief

ISBN: 978-1-59707-707-1 paperback edition
ISBN: 978-1-59707-708-8 hardcover edition

Papercutz books may be purchased for business or promotional use. For information on bulk purchases please contact Macmillan
Corporate and Premium Sales Department at (800) 221-7945 x5442.

Printed in the USA
January 2014 by Lifetouch Printing
5126 Forest Hills Ct.
Loves Park, IL 61111

Distributed by Macmillan
First Printing

FSC
www.fsc.org
MIX
Paper from
responsible sources
FSC® C112431

MEET THE MASTERS OF SPINJITZU

JAY

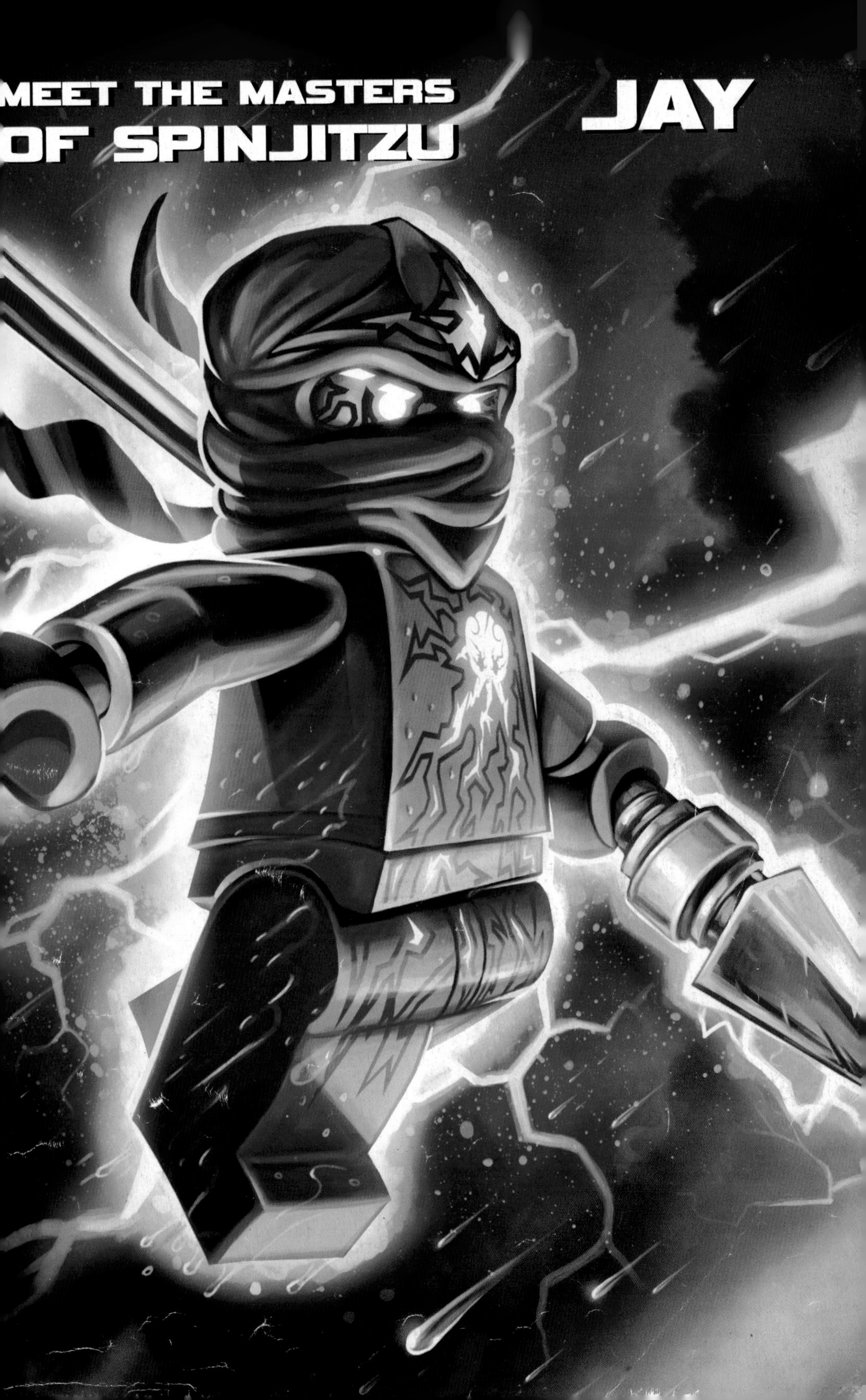

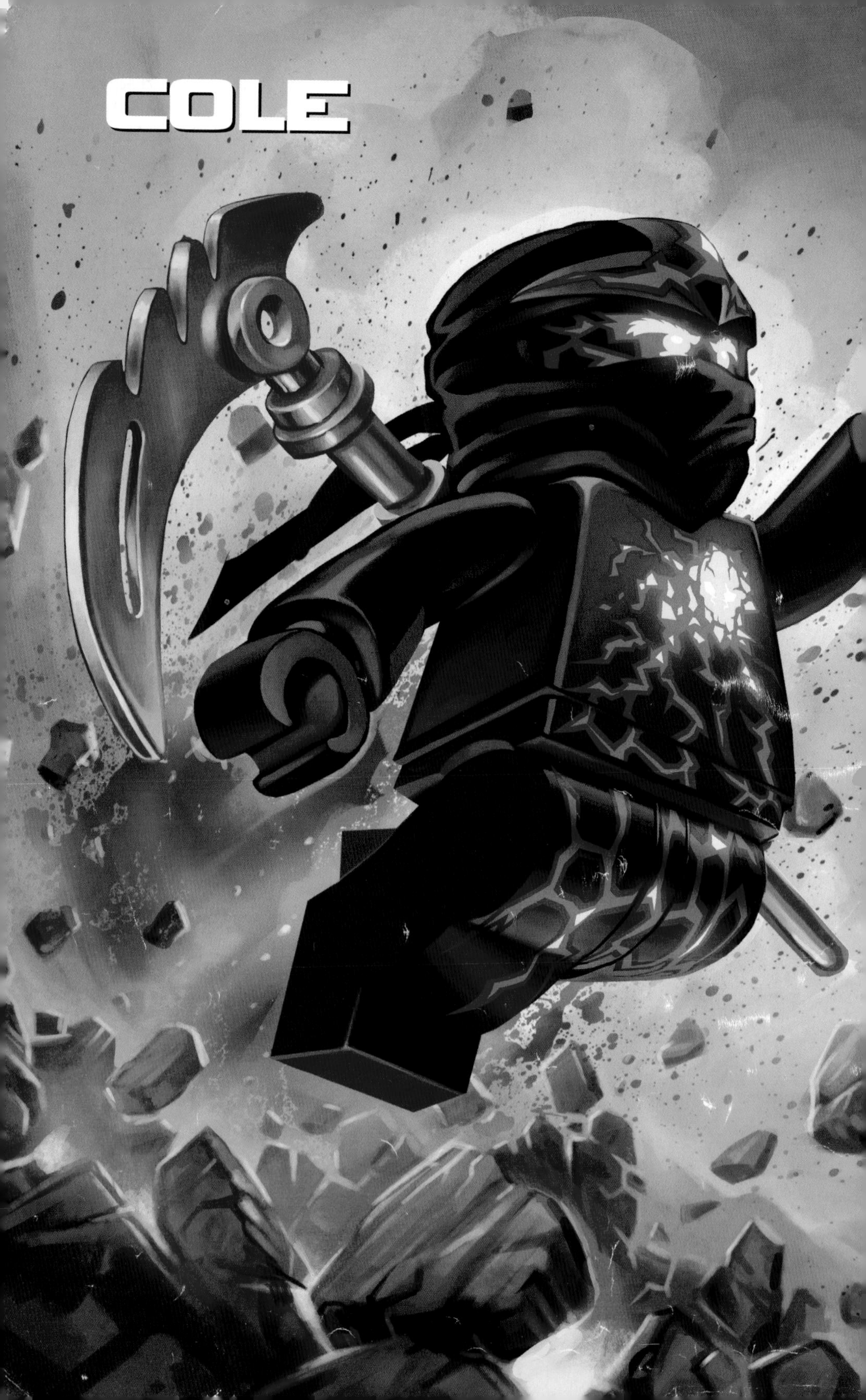
COLE

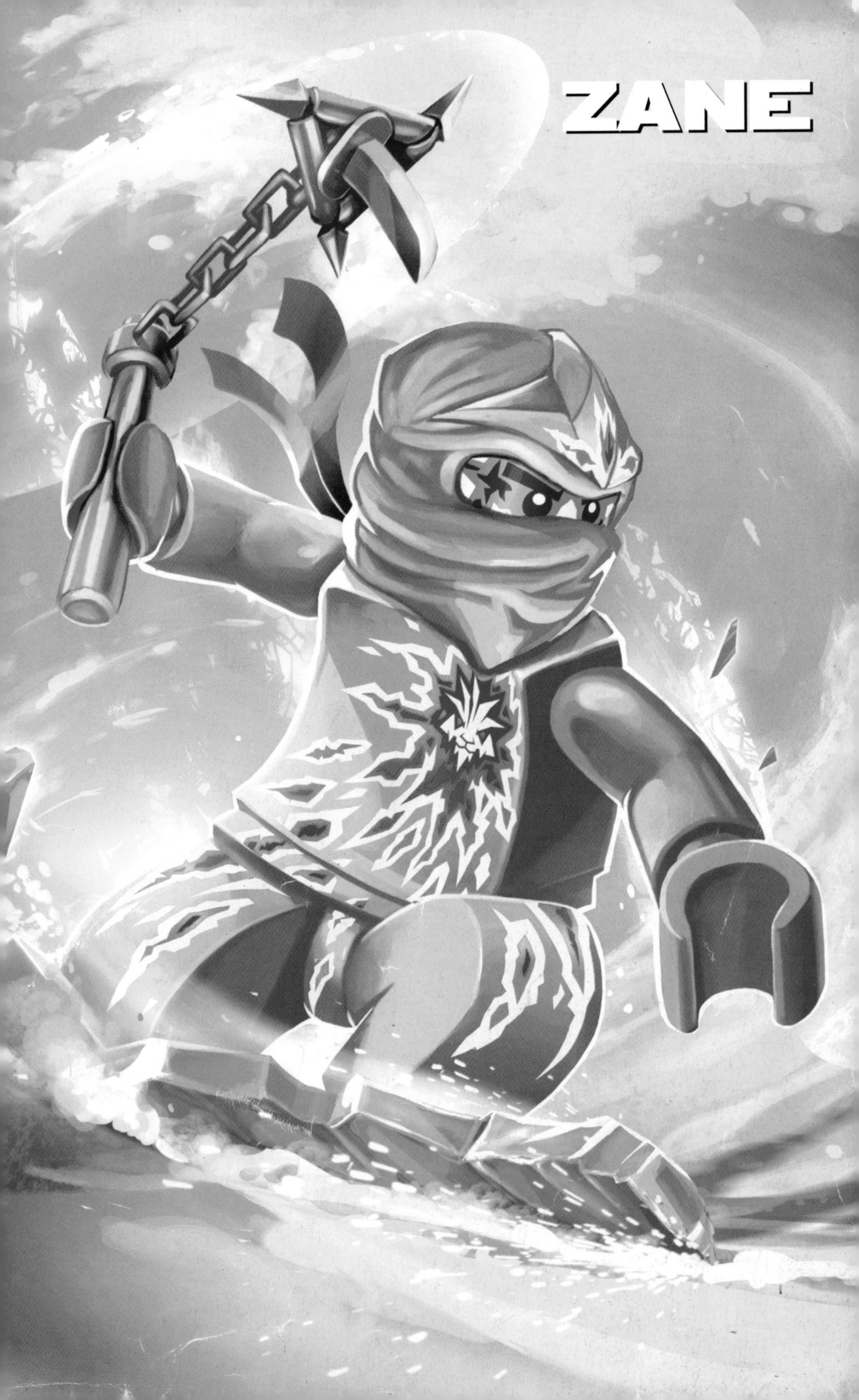
ZANE

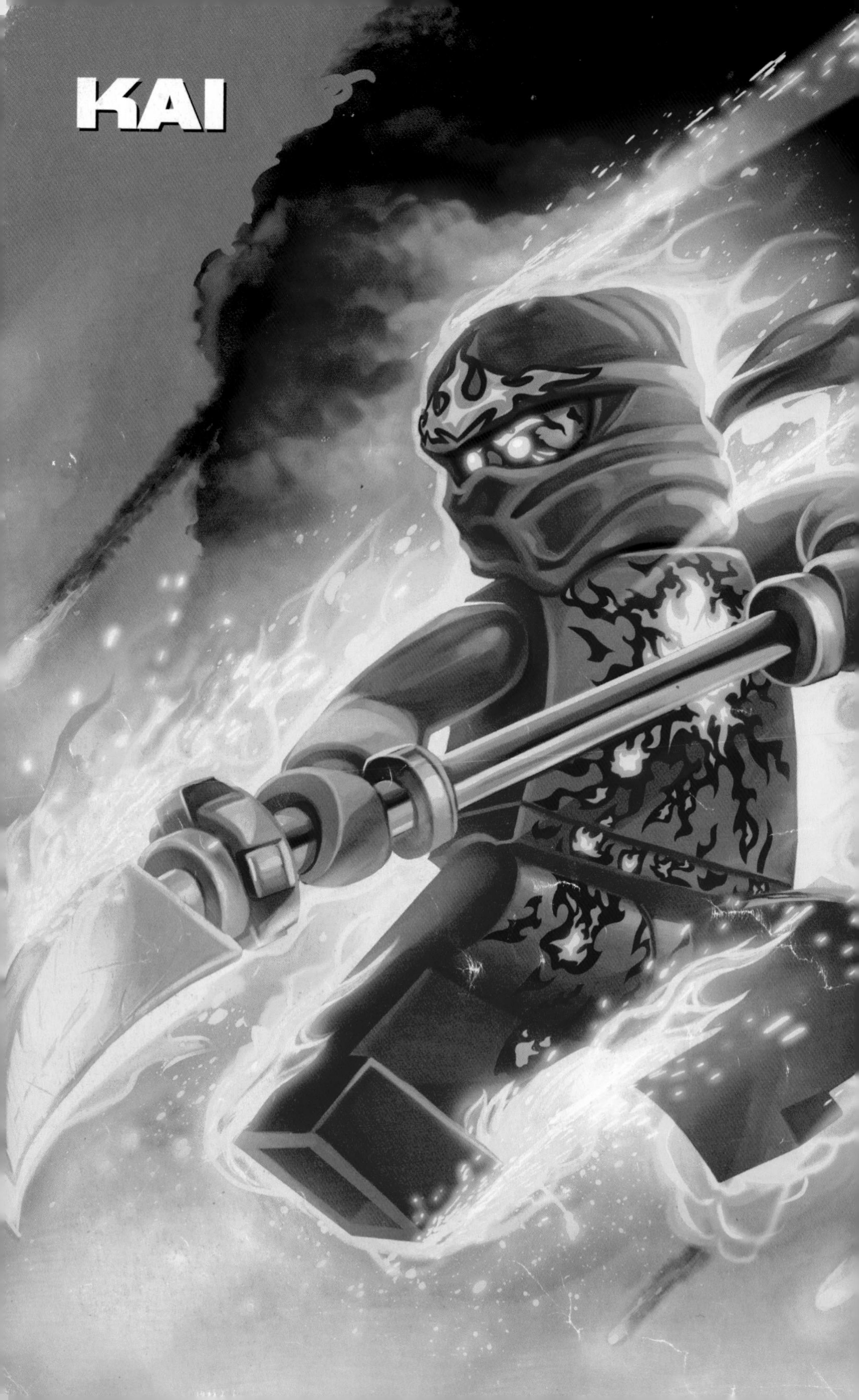
KAI

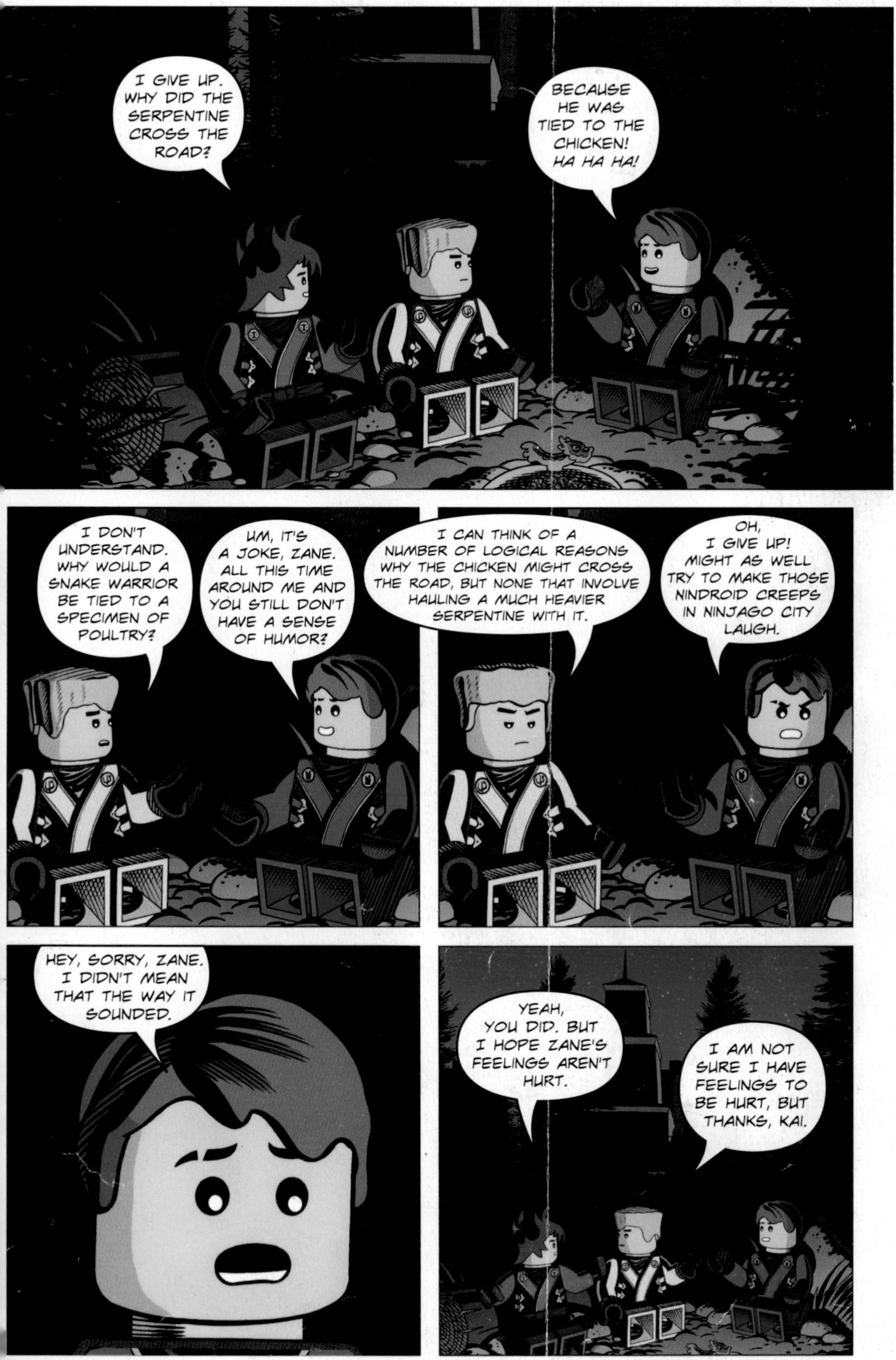
I GIVE UP. WHY DID THE SERPENTINE CROSS THE ROAD?
BECAUSE HE WAS TIED TO THE CHICKEN! HA HA HA!
I DON'T UNDERSTAND. WHY WOULD A SNAKE WARRIOR BE TIED TO A SPECIMEN OF POULTRY?
UM, IT'S A JOKE, ZANE. ALL THIS TIME AROUND ME AND YOU STILL DON'T HAVE A SENSE OF HUMOR?
I CAN THINK OF A NUMBER OF LOGICAL REASONS WHY THE CHICKEN MIGHT CROSS THE ROAD, BUT NONE THAT INVOLVE HAULING A MUCH HEAVIER SERPENTINE WITH IT.
OH, I GIVE UP! MIGHT AS WELL TRY TO MAKE THOSE NINDROID CREEPS IN NINJAGO CITY LAUGH.
HEY, SORRY, ZANE. I DIDN'T MEAN THAT THE WAY IT SOUNDED.
YEAH, YOU DID. BUT I HOPE ZANE'S FEELINGS AREN'T HURT.
I AM NOT SURE I HAVE FEELINGS TO BE HURT, BUT THANKS, KAI.

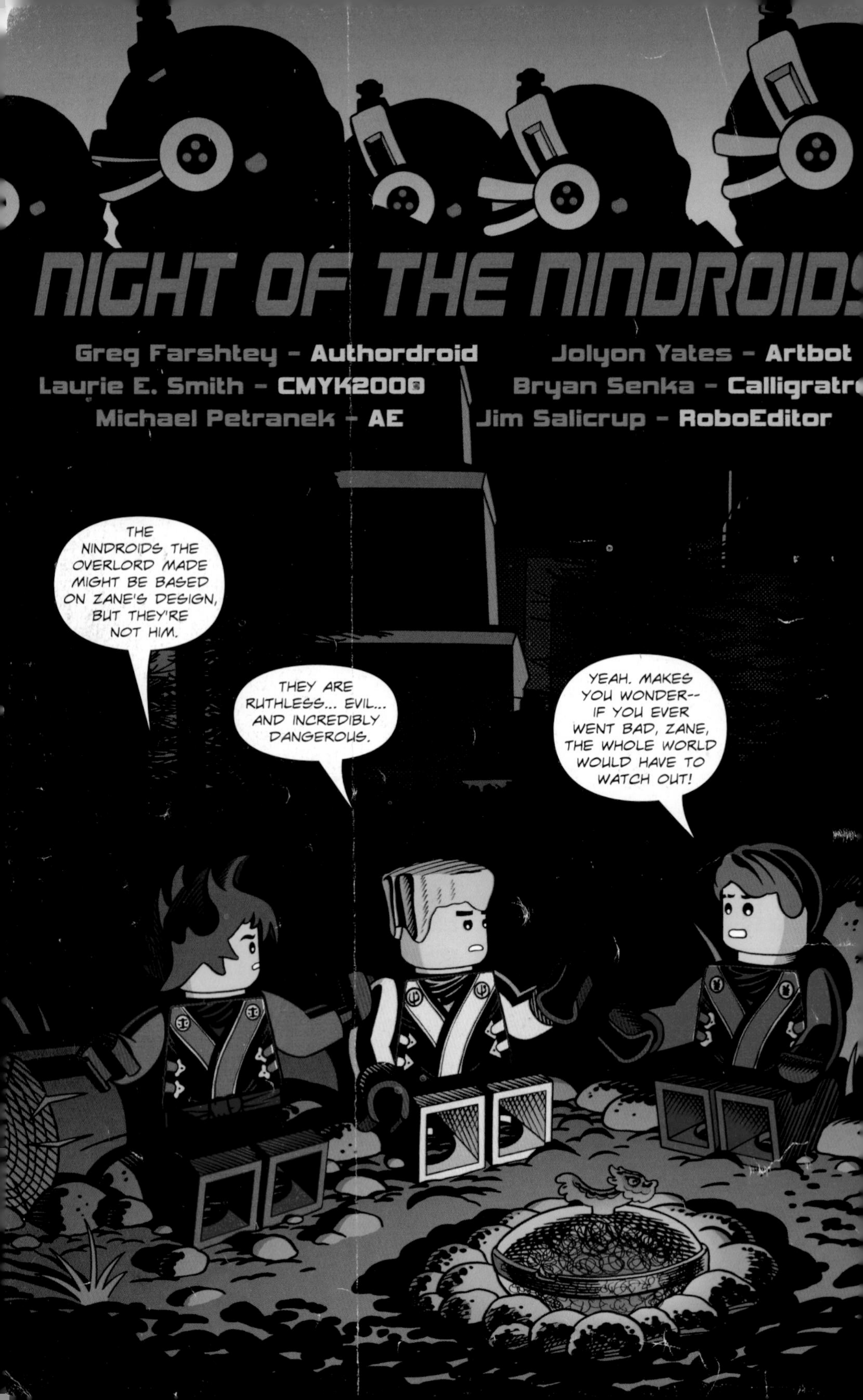
NIGHT OF THE NINDROIDS
Greg Farshtey - Authordroid
Jolyon Yates - Artbot
Laurie E. Smith - CMYK2000
Bryan Senka - Calligratr
Michael Petranek - AE
Jim Salicrup - RoboEditor
THE NINDROIDS THE OVERLORD MADE MIGHT BE BASED ON ZANE'S DESIGN, BUT THEY'RE NOT HIM.
THEY ARE RUTHLESS... EVIL... AND INCREDIBLY DANGEROUS.
YEAH. MAKES YOU WONDER-- IF YOU EVER WENT BAD, ZANE, THE WHOLE WORLD WOULD HAVE TO WATCH OUT!

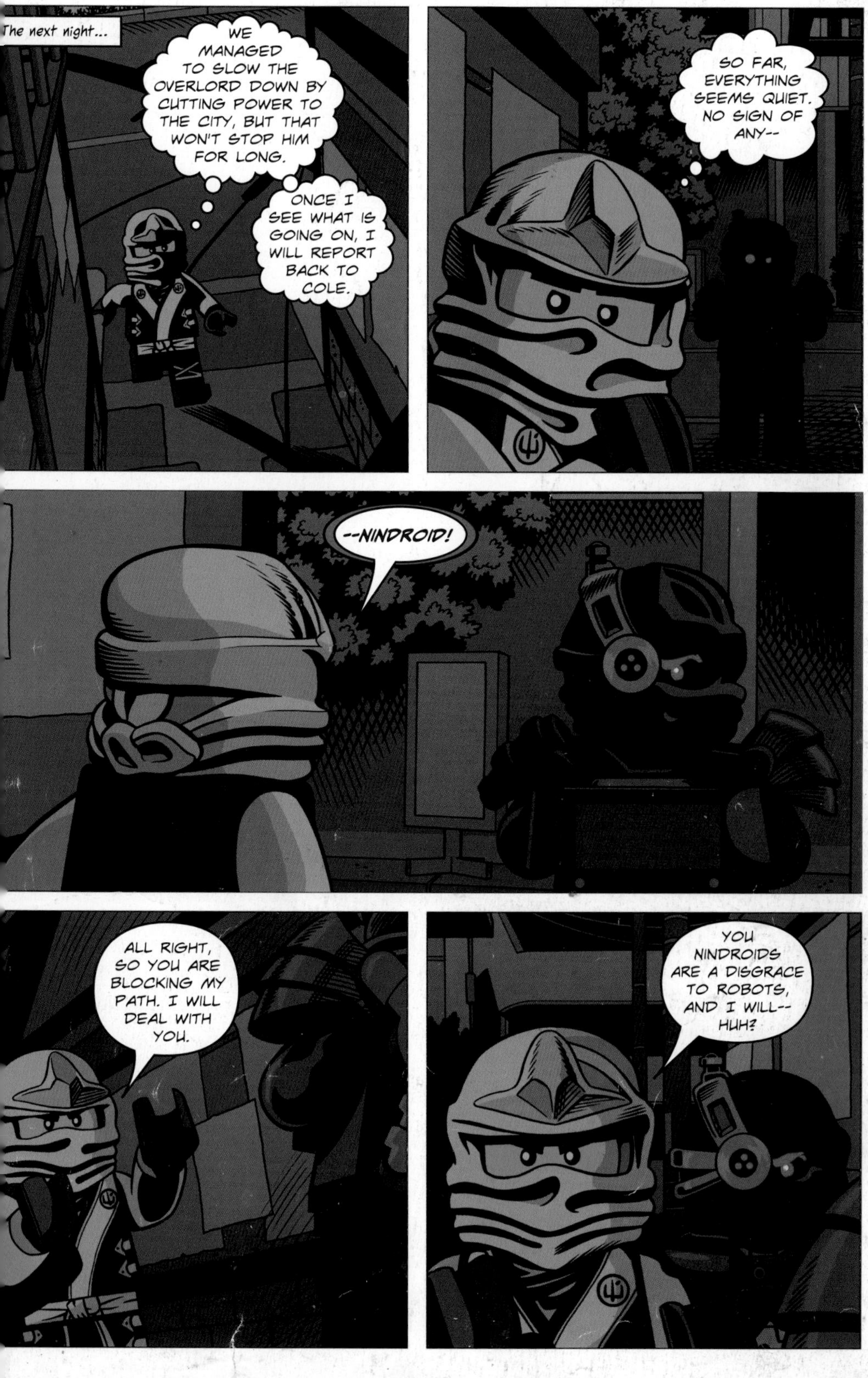
The next night...
WE MANAGED TO SLOW THE OVERLORD DOWN BY CUTTING POWER TO THE CITY, BUT THAT WON'T STOP HIM FOR LONG.
ONCE I SEE WHAT IS GOING ON, I WILL REPORT BACK TO COLE.
SO FAR, EVERYTHING SEEMS QUIET. NO SIGN OF ANY--
--NINDROID!
ALL RIGHT, SO YOU ARE BLOCKING MY PATH. I WILL DEAL WITH YOU.
YOU NINDROIDS ARE A DISGRACE TO ROBOTS, AND I WILL-- HUH?

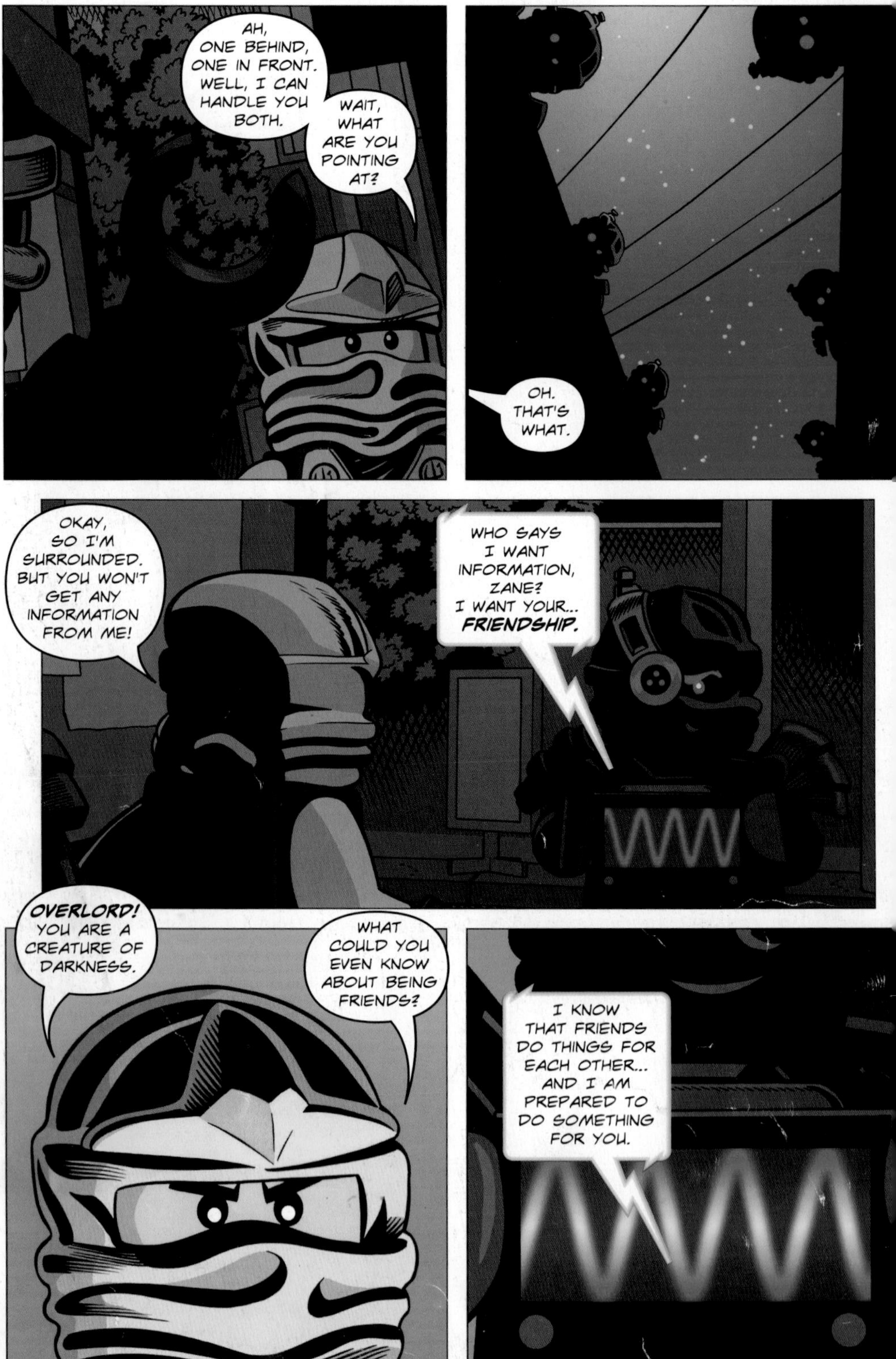
AH, ONE BEHIND, ONE IN FRONT. WELL, I CAN HANDLE YOU BOTH.
WAIT, WHAT ARE YOU POINTING AT?
OH. THAT'S WHAT.
OKAY, SO I'M SURROUNDED. BUT YOU WON'T GET ANY INFORMATION FROM ME!
WHO SAYS I WANT INFORMATION, ZANE? I WANT YOUR... FRIENDSHIP.
OVERLORD! YOU ARE A CREATURE OF DARKNESS.
WHAT COULD YOU EVEN KNOW ABOUT BEING FRIENDS?
I KNOW THAT FRIENDS DO THINGS FOR EACH OTHER... AND I AM PREPARED TO DO SOMETHING FOR YOU.

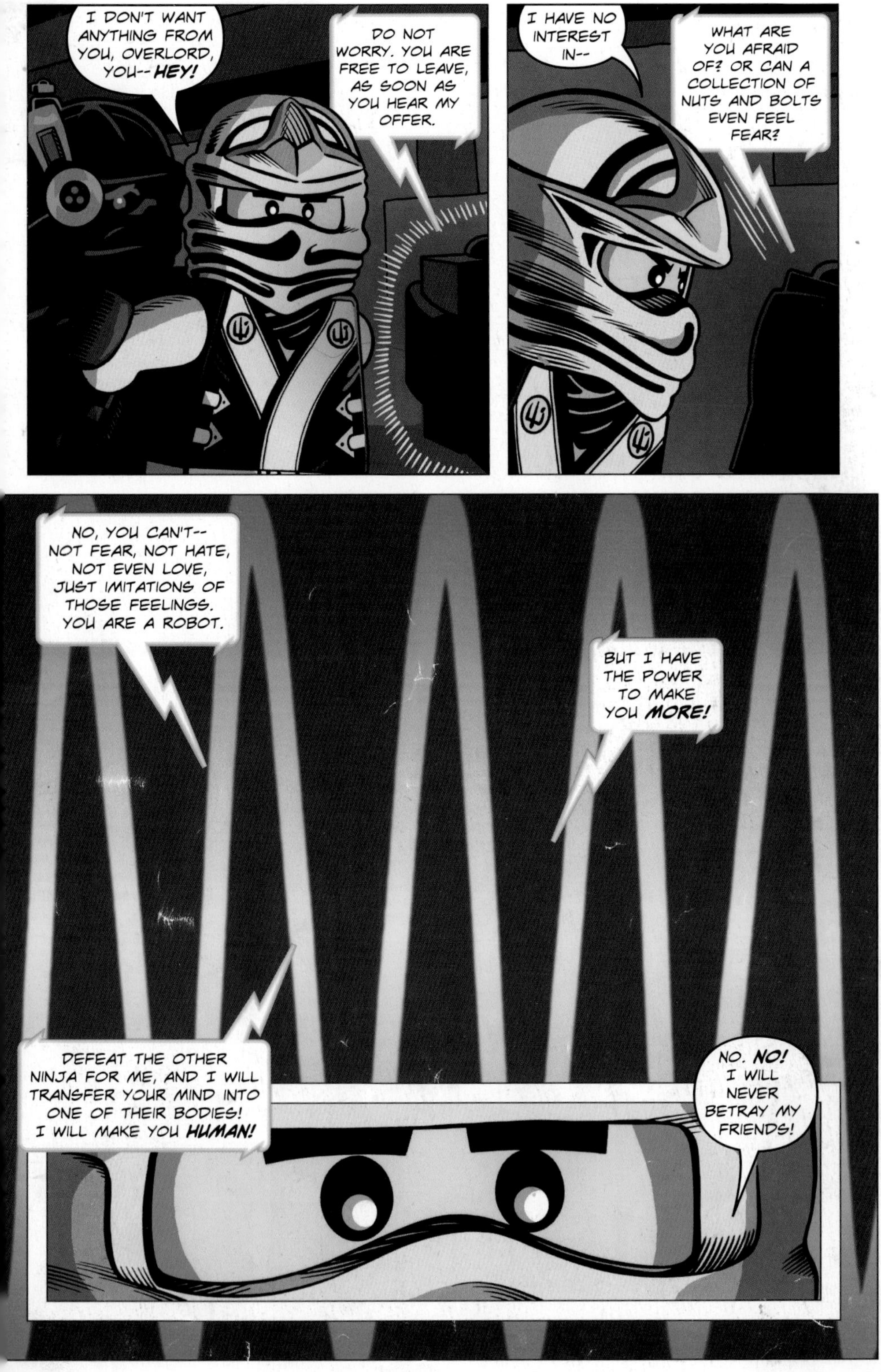
I DON'T WANT ANYTHING FROM YOU, OVERLORD, YOU--**HEY!**
DO NOT WORRY. YOU ARE FREE TO LEAVE, AS SOON AS YOU HEAR MY OFFER.
I HAVE NO INTEREST IN--
WHAT ARE YOU AFRAID OF? OR CAN A COLLECTION OF NUTS AND BOLTS EVEN FEEL FEAR?
NO, YOU CAN'T--NOT FEAR, NOT HATE, NOT EVEN LOVE, JUST IMITATIONS OF THOSE FEELINGS. YOU ARE A ROBOT.
BUT I HAVE THE POWER TO MAKE YOU **MORE!**
DEFEAT THE OTHER NINJA FOR ME, AND I WILL TRANSFER YOUR MIND INTO ONE OF THEIR BODIES! I WILL MAKE YOU **HUMAN!**
NO. **NO!** I WILL NEVER BETRAY MY FRIENDS!

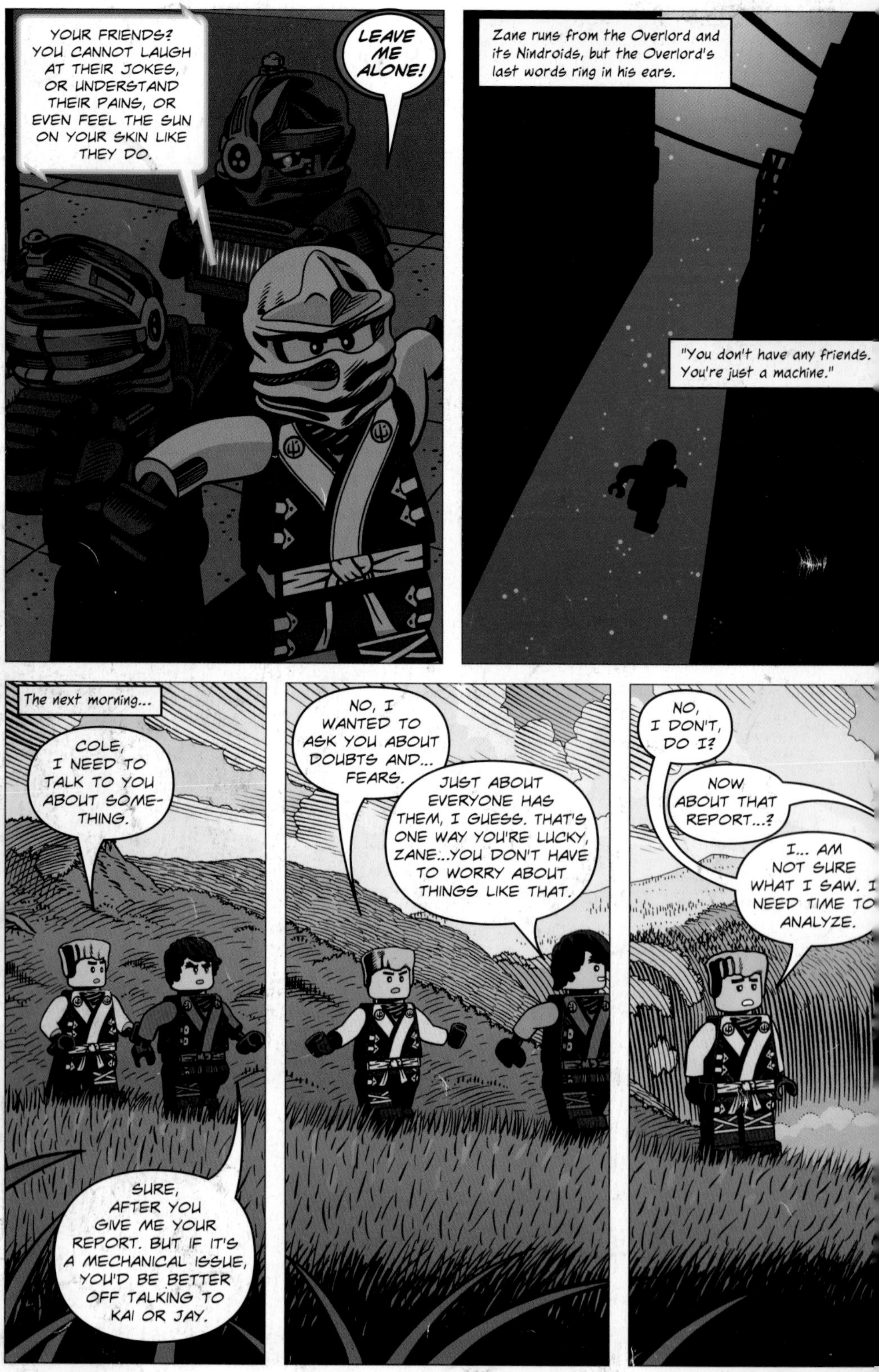
YOUR FRIENDS? YOU CANNOT LAUGH AT THEIR JOKES, OR UNDERSTAND THEIR PAINS, OR EVEN FEEL THE SUN ON YOUR SKIN LIKE THEY DO.
LEAVE ME ALONE!
Zane runs from the Overlord and its Nindroids, but the Overlord's last words ring in his ears.
"You don't have any friends. You're just a machine."
The next morning...
COLE, I NEED TO TALK TO YOU ABOUT SOME-THING.
SURE, AFTER YOU GIVE ME YOUR REPORT. BUT IF IT'S A MECHANICAL ISSUE, YOU'D BE BETTER OFF TALKING TO KAI OR JAY.
NO, I WANTED TO ASK YOU ABOUT DOUBTS AND... FEARS.
JUST ABOUT EVERYONE HAS THEM, I GUESS. THAT'S ONE WAY YOU'RE LUCKY, ZANE...YOU DON'T HAVE TO WORRY ABOUT THINGS LIKE THAT.
NO, I DON'T, DO I?
NOW ABOUT THAT REPORT...?
I... AM NOT SURE WHAT I SAW. I NEED TIME TO ANALYZE.

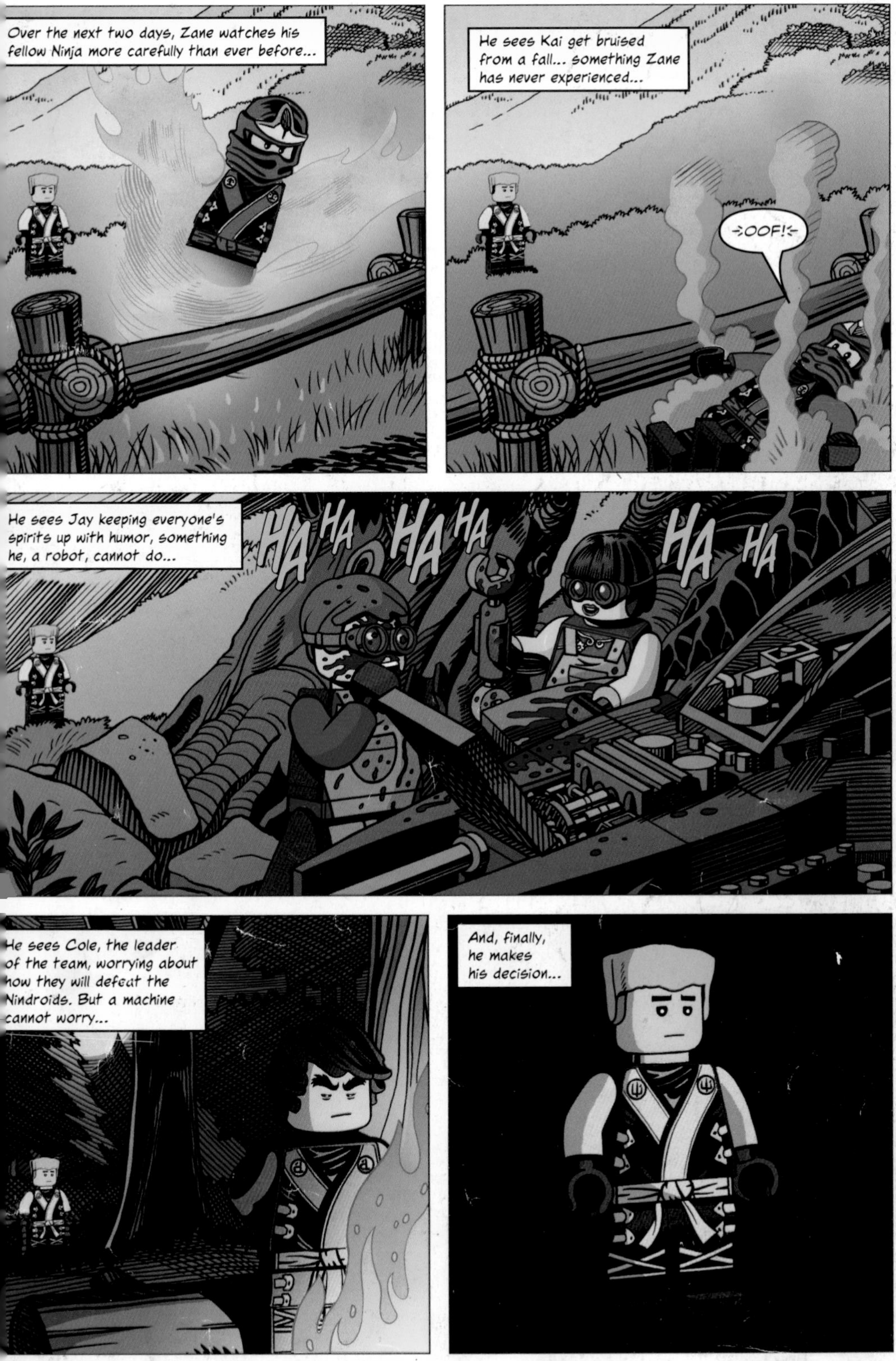
Over the next two days, Zane watches his fellow Ninja more carefully than ever before...
He sees Kai get bruised from a fall... something Zane has never experienced...
OOF!
He sees Jay keeping everyone's spirits up with humor, something he, a robot, cannot do...
HA HA HA HA
HA HA
He sees Cole, the leader of the team, worrying about how they will defeat the Nindroids. But a machine cannot worry...
And, finally, he makes his decision...

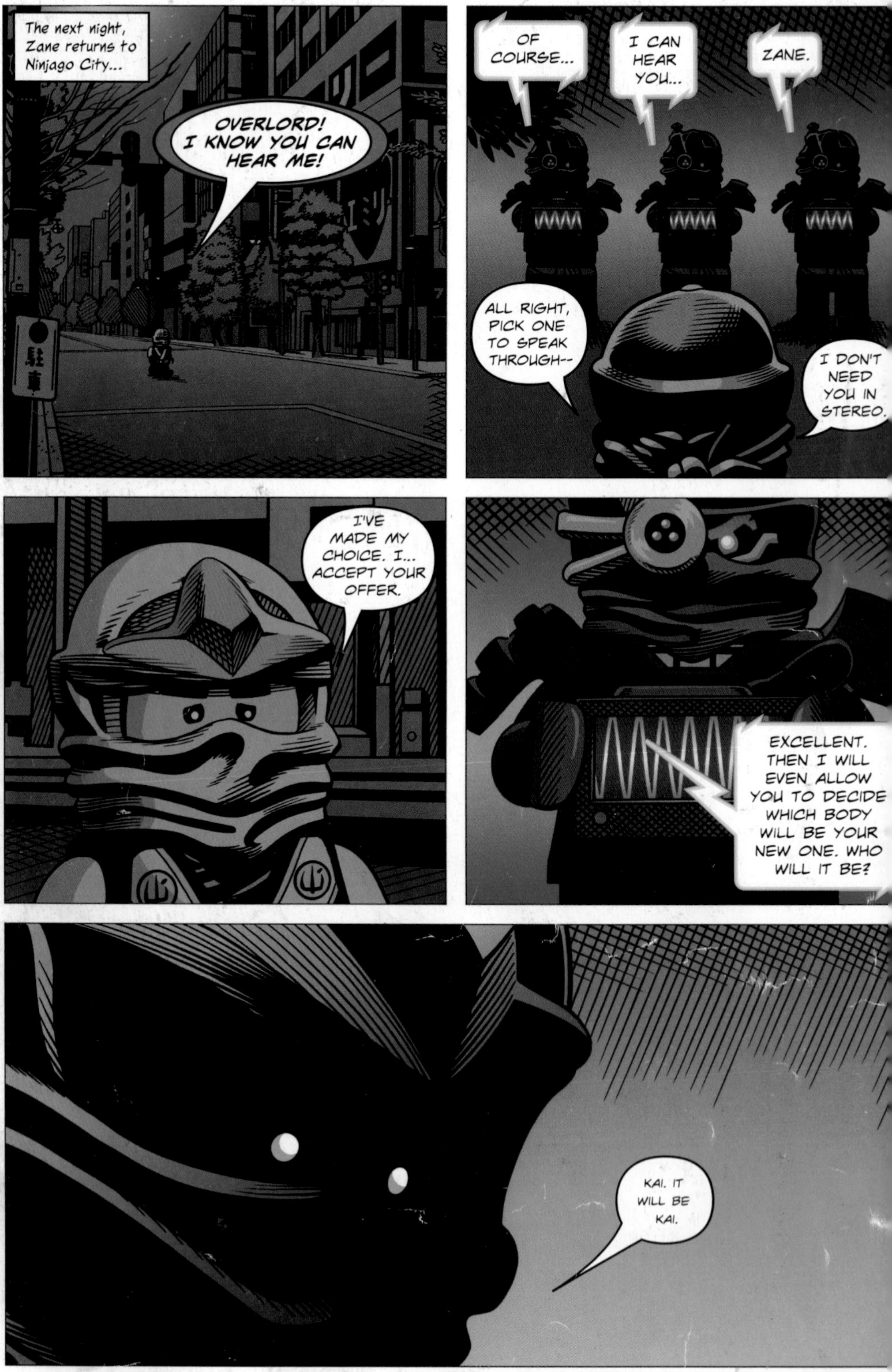
The next night, Zane returns to Ninjago City...
OVERLORD! I KNOW YOU CAN HEAR ME!
OF COURSE...
I CAN HEAR YOU...
ZANE.
ALL RIGHT, PICK ONE TO SPEAK THROUGH--
I DON'T NEED YOU IN STEREO.
I'VE MADE MY CHOICE. I... ACCEPT YOUR OFFER.
EXCELLENT. THEN I WILL EVEN ALLOW YOU TO DECIDE WHICH BODY WILL BE YOUR NEW ONE. WHO WILL IT BE?
KAI. IT WILL BE KAI.

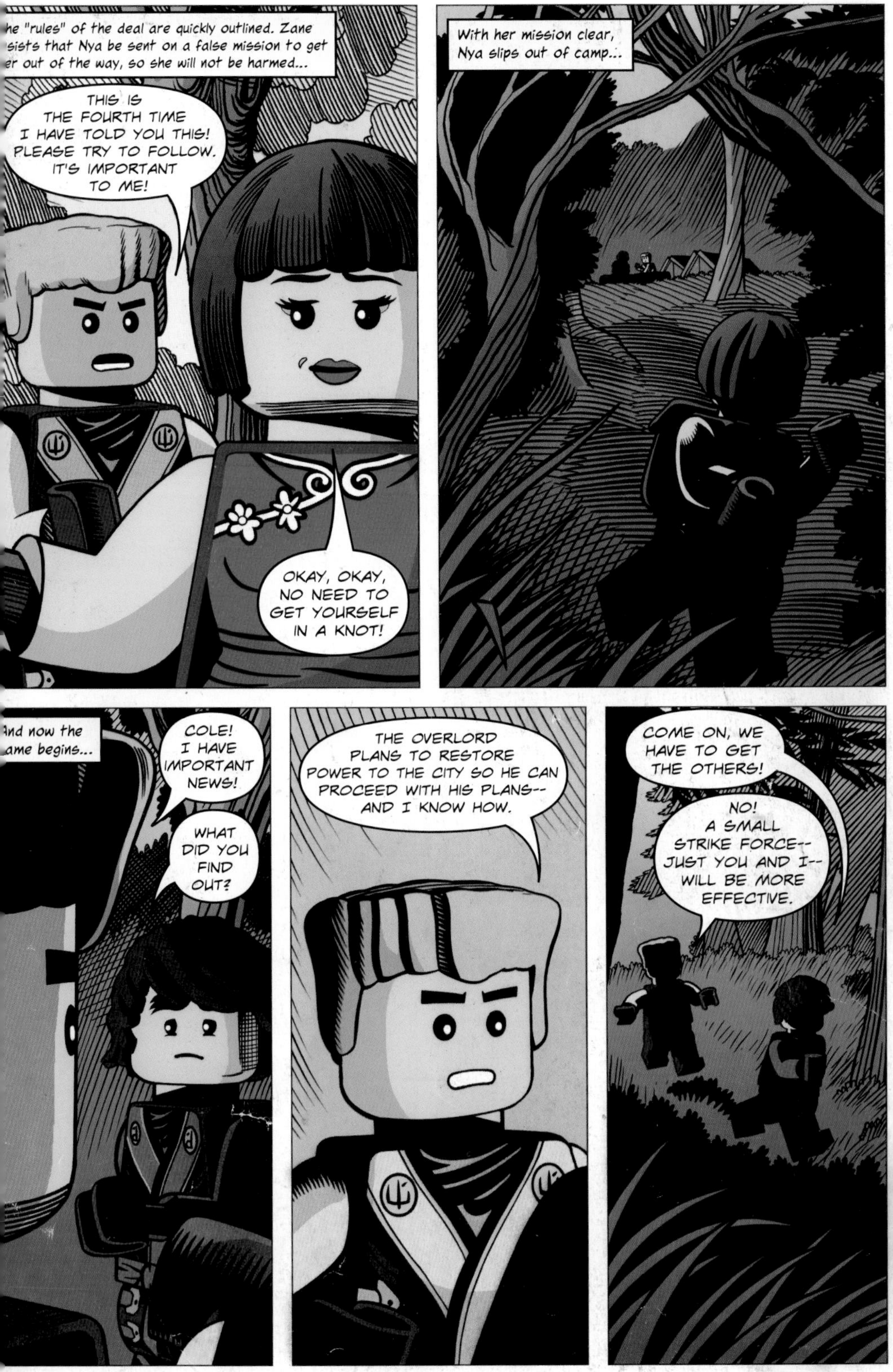
he "rules" of the deal are quickly outlined. Zane
sists that Nya be sent on a false mission to get
er out of the way, so she will not be harmed...
THIS IS THE FOURTH TIME I HAVE TOLD YOU THIS! PLEASE TRY TO FOLLOW. IT'S IMPORTANT TO ME!
OKAY, OKAY, NO NEED TO GET YOURSELF IN A KNOT!
With her mission clear, Nya slips out of camp...
nd now the
ame begins...
COLE! I HAVE IMPORTANT NEWS!
WHAT DID YOU FIND OUT?
THE OVERLORD PLANS TO RESTORE POWER TO THE CITY SO HE CAN PROCEED WITH HIS PLANS-- AND I KNOW HOW.
COME ON, WE HAVE TO GET THE OTHERS!
NO! A SMALL STRIKE FORCE-- JUST YOU AND I-- WILL BE MORE EFFECTIVE.

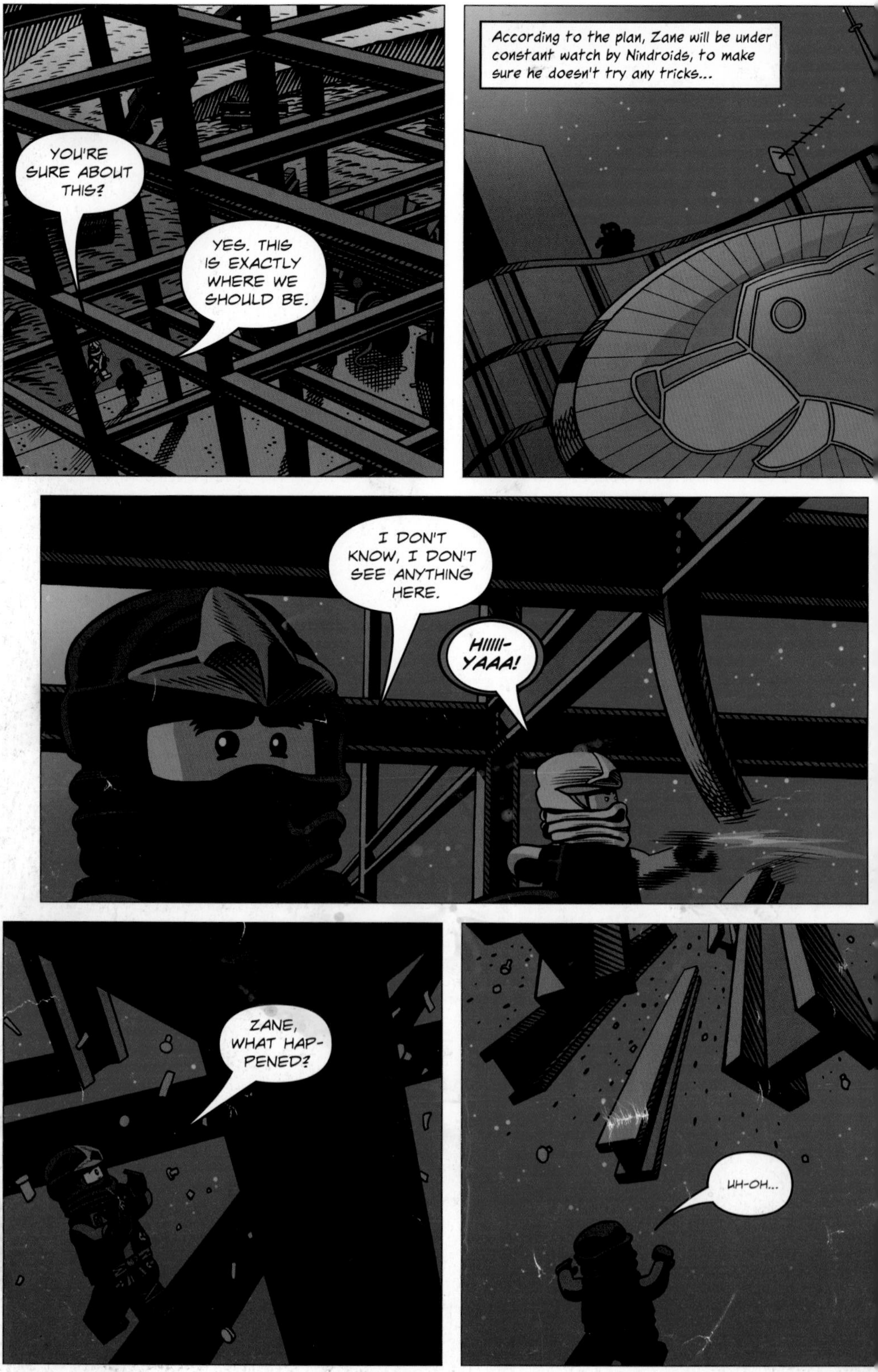
YOU'RE SURE ABOUT THIS?
YES. THIS IS EXACTLY WHERE WE SHOULD BE.
According to the plan, Zane will be under constant watch by Nindroids, to make sure he doesn't try any tricks...
I DON'T KNOW, I DON'T SEE ANYTHING HERE.
HIIIII-YAAA!
ZANE, WHAT HAP-PENED?
UH-OH...

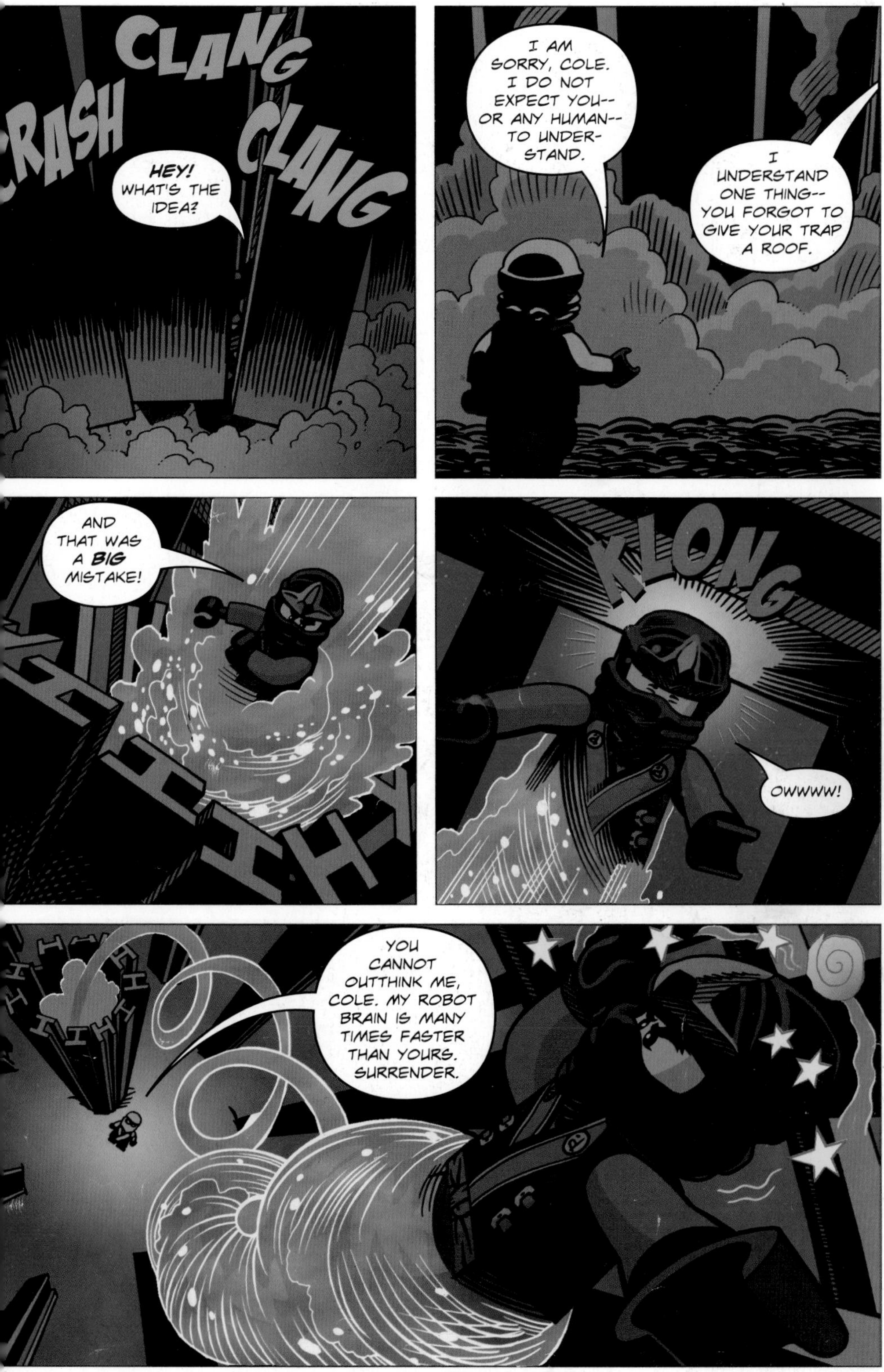
CRASH
CLANG
CLANG
HEY! WHAT'S THE IDEA?
I AM SORRY, COLE. I DO NOT EXPECT YOU-- OR ANY HUMAN-- TO UNDER-STAND.
I UNDERSTAND ONE THING-- YOU FORGOT TO GIVE YOUR TRAP A ROOF.
AND THAT WAS A BIG MISTAKE!
KLONG
OWWWW!
YOU CANNOT OUTTHINK ME, COLE. MY ROBOT BRAIN IS MANY TIMES FASTER THAN YOURS. SURRENDER.

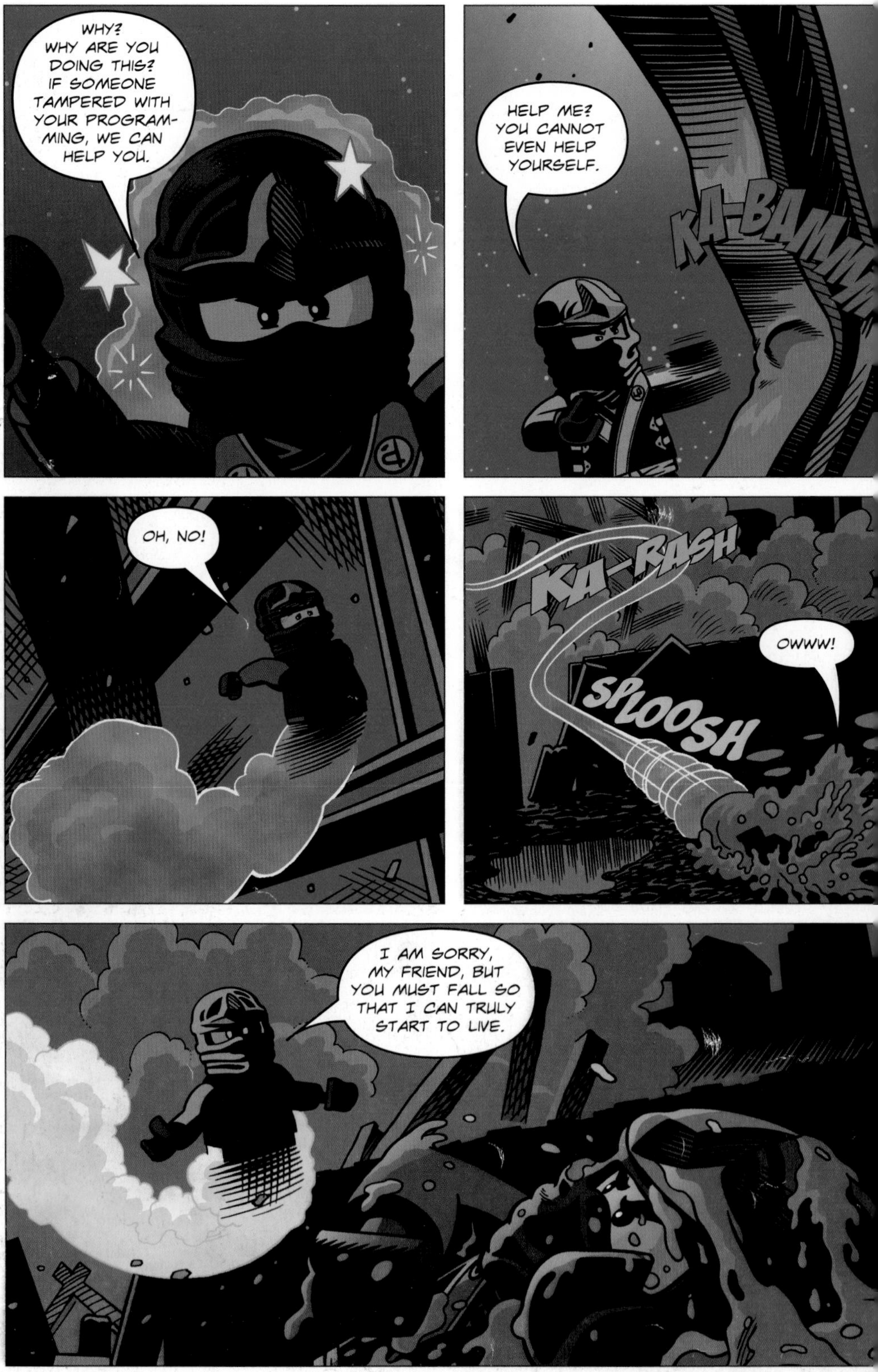
WHY? WHY ARE YOU DOING THIS? IF SOMEONE TAMPERED WITH YOUR PROGRAMMING, WE CAN HELP YOU.
HELP ME? YOU CANNOT EVEN HELP YOURSELF.
KA-BAMM
OH, NO!
KA-RASH
OWWW!
SPLOOSH
I AM SORRY, MY FRIEND, BUT YOU MUST FALL SO THAT I CAN TRULY START TO LIVE.

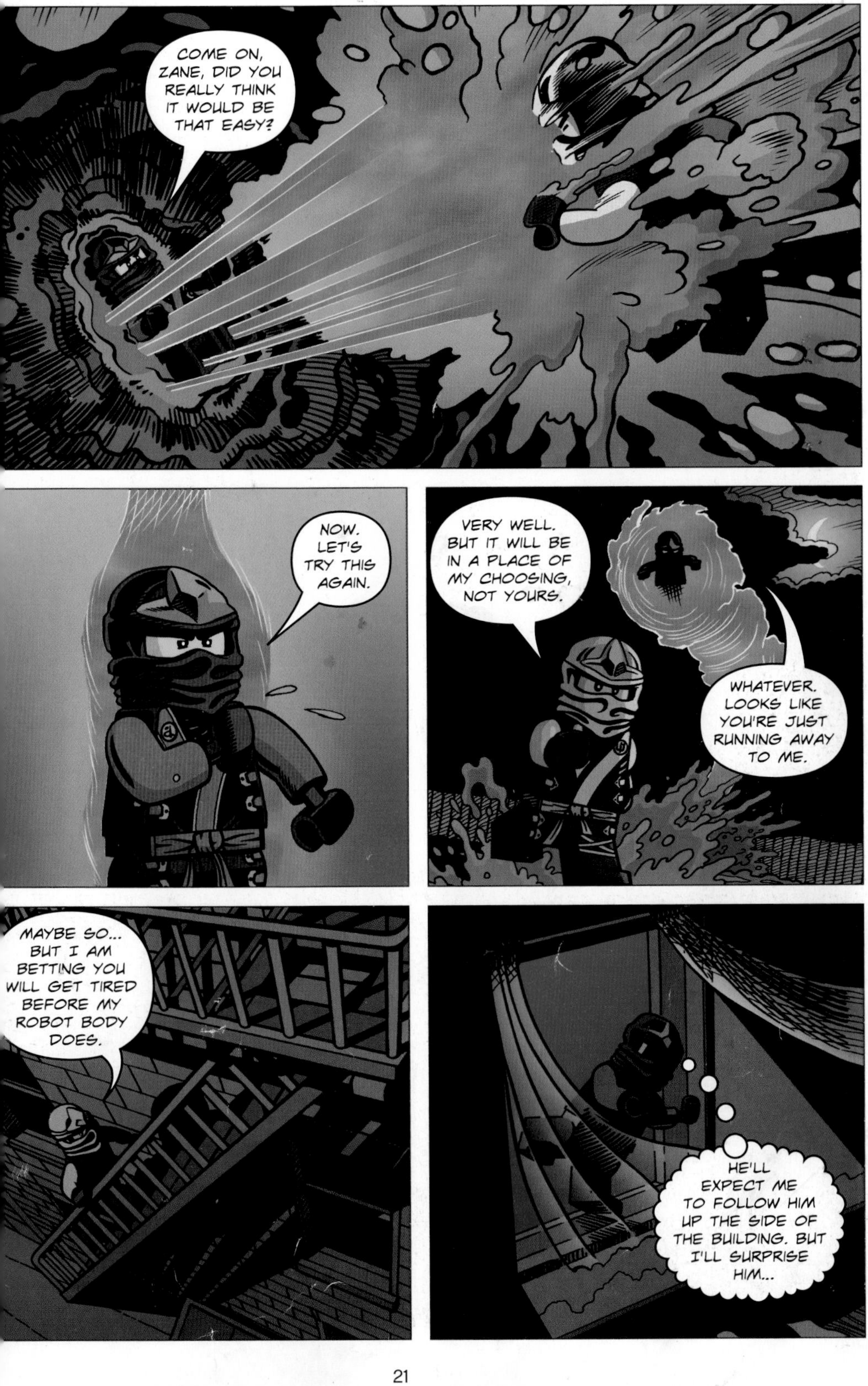
COME ON, ZANE, DID YOU REALLY THINK IT WOULD BE THAT EASY?
NOW. LET'S TRY THIS AGAIN.
VERY WELL. BUT IT WILL BE IN A PLACE OF MY CHOOSING, NOT YOURS.
WHATEVER. LOOKS LIKE YOU'RE JUST RUNNING AWAY TO ME.
MAYBE SO... BUT I AM BETTING YOU WILL GET TIRED BEFORE MY ROBOT BODY DOES.
HE'LL EXPECT ME TO FOLLOW HIM UP THE SIDE OF THE BUILDING. BUT I'LL SURPRISE HIM...

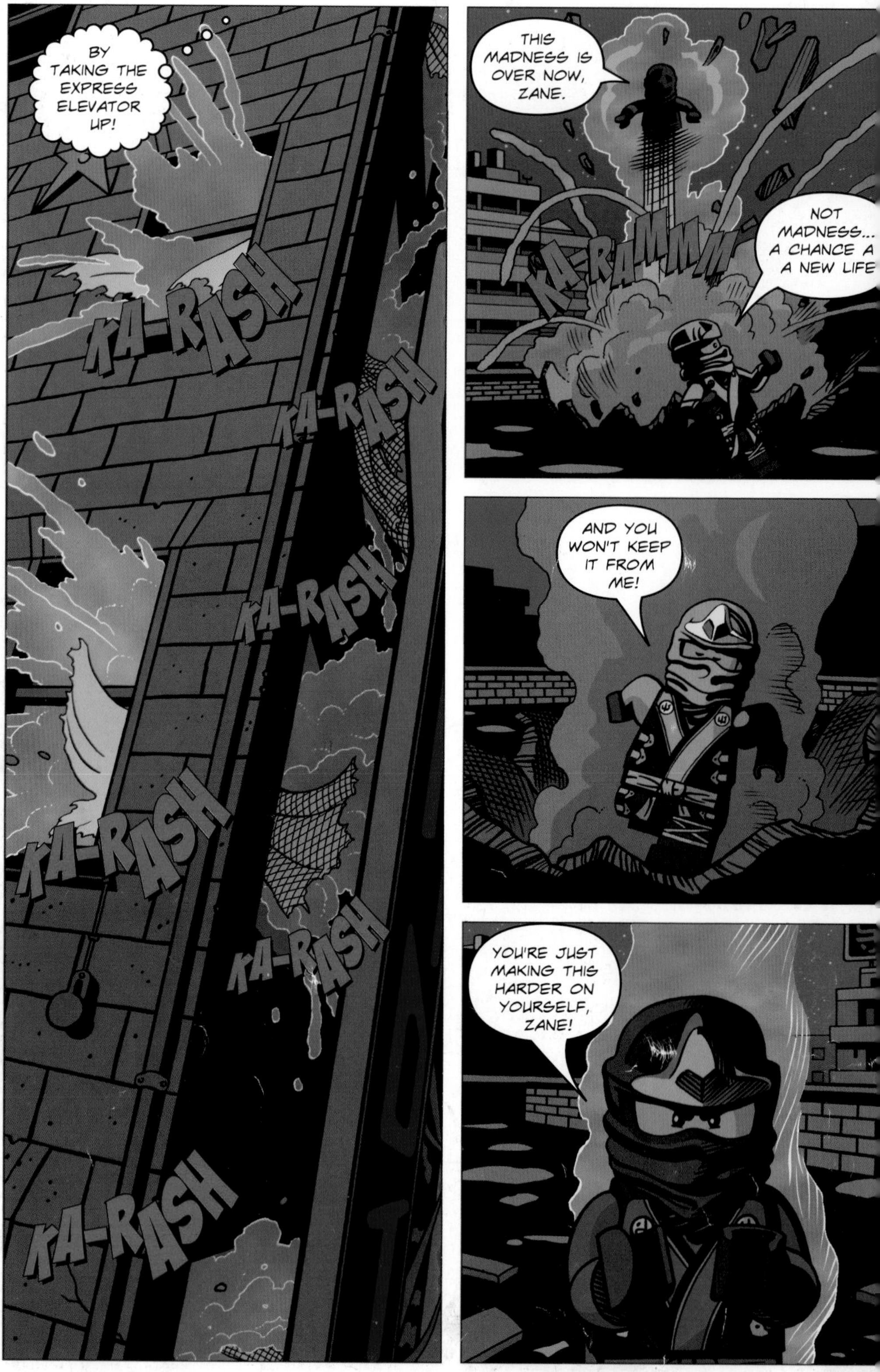
BY TAKING THE EXPRESS ELEVATOR UP!
KA-RASH
KA-RASH
KA-RASH
KA-RASH
KA-RASH
KA-RASH
THIS MADNESS IS OVER NOW, ZANE.
KA-RAMMMM
NOT MADNESS... A CHANCE A A NEW LIFE
AND YOU WON'T KEEP IT FROM ME!
YOU'RE JUST MAKING THIS HARDER ON YOURSELF, ZANE!

Doing his best to stay silent, Cole searches the darkness for Zane...

..And finds him!

COLE. IT IS TIME TO END THIS.

AT LEAST, WE AGREE ON SOMETHING.

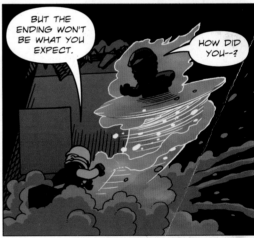

BUT THE ENDING WON'T BE WHAT YOU EXPECT.

HOW DID YOU--?

A SMALL ELECTRICAL CHARGE, JUST ENOUGH TO SPEED UP YOUR SPIN BEYOND YOUR ABILITY TO CONTROL IT.

KZZZAKKK

ZANE, WHAT DID YOU DO? I'M SPINNING TOO FAST!

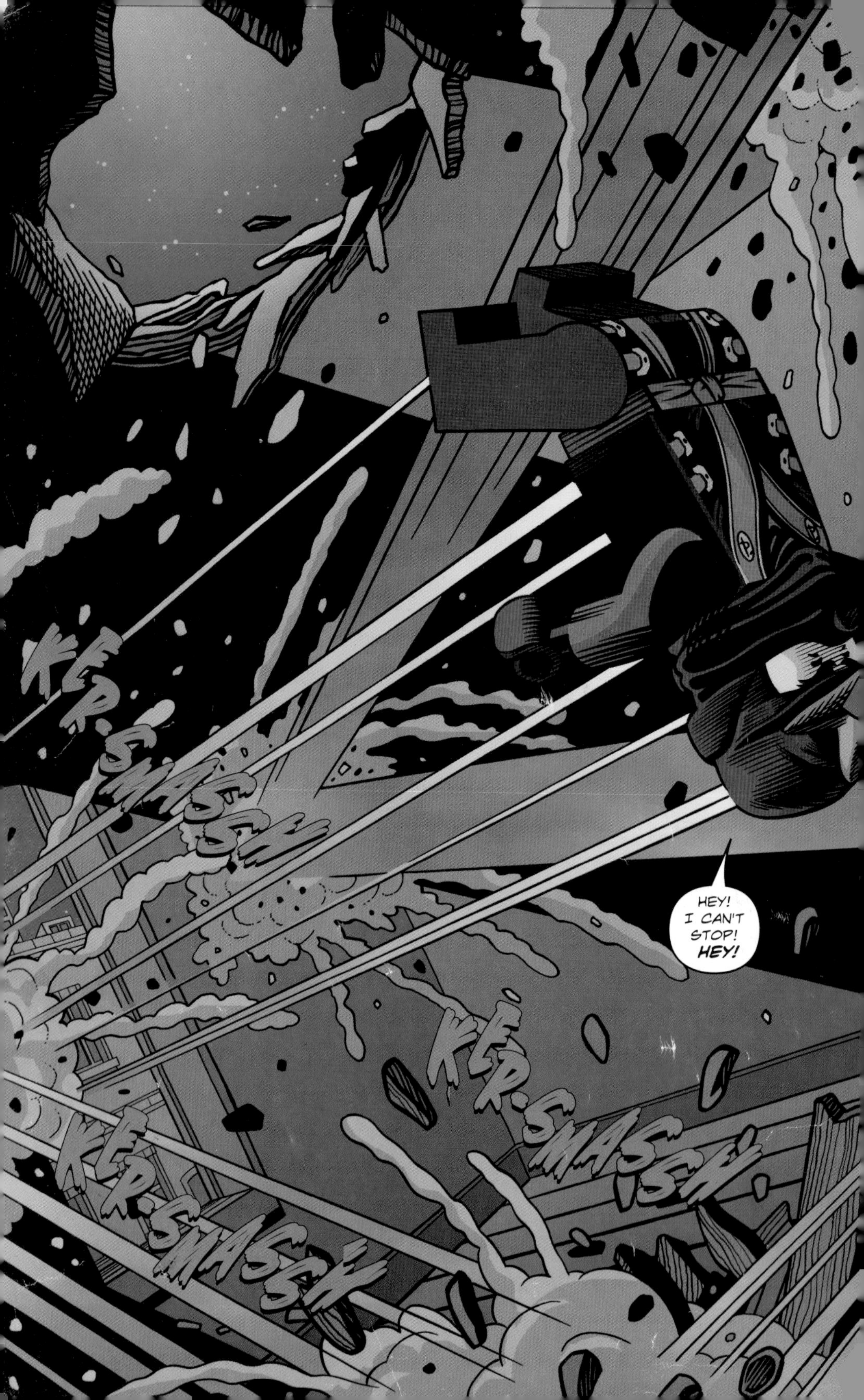
KER-SMASSH
HEY! I CAN'T STOP! **HEY!**
KER-SMASSH!
KER-SMASSH!

CRASH

OH, YOU MISSED THAT LAST TURN.

THIS TIME, I'LL MAKE SURE YOU'RE CAPTURED.

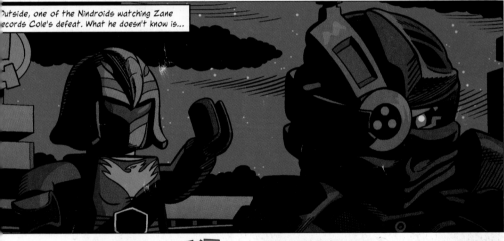

Outside, one of the Nindroids watching Zane records Cole's defeat. What he doesn't know is...

...he is about to meet his own...

KA-KRUNNG

THE ONLY GOOD NINDROID IS AN UNCONSCIOUS NINDROID.

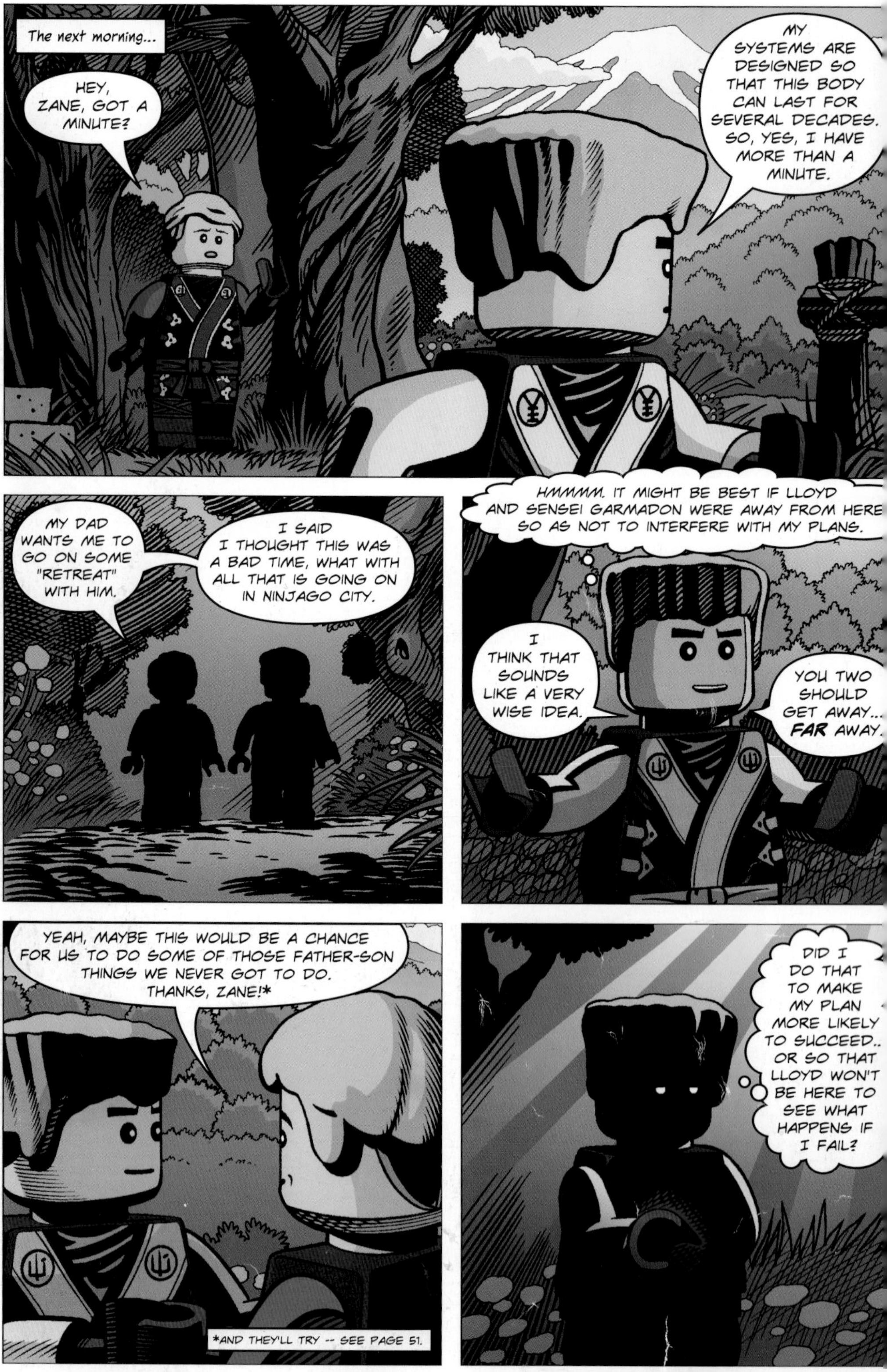
The next morning...
HEY, ZANE, GOT A MINUTE?
MY SYSTEMS ARE DESIGNED SO THAT THIS BODY CAN LAST FOR SEVERAL DECADES. SO, YES, I HAVE MORE THAN A MINUTE.
MY DAD WANTS ME TO GO ON SOME "RETREAT" WITH HIM.
I SAID I THOUGHT THIS WAS A BAD TIME, WHAT WITH ALL THAT IS GOING ON IN NINJAGO CITY.
HMMMM. IT MIGHT BE BEST IF LLOYD AND SENSEI GARMADON WERE AWAY FROM HERE SO AS NOT TO INTERFERE WITH MY PLANS.
I THINK THAT SOUNDS LIKE A VERY WISE IDEA.
YOU TWO SHOULD GET AWAY... FAR AWAY.
YEAH, MAYBE THIS WOULD BE A CHANCE FOR US TO DO SOME OF THOSE FATHER-SON THINGS WE NEVER GOT TO DO. THANKS, ZANE!*
*AND THEY'LL TRY -- SEE PAGE 51.
DID I DO THAT TO MAKE MY PLAN MORE LIKELY TO SUCCEED.. OR SO THAT LLOYD WON'T BE HERE TO SEE WHAT HAPPENS IF I FAIL?

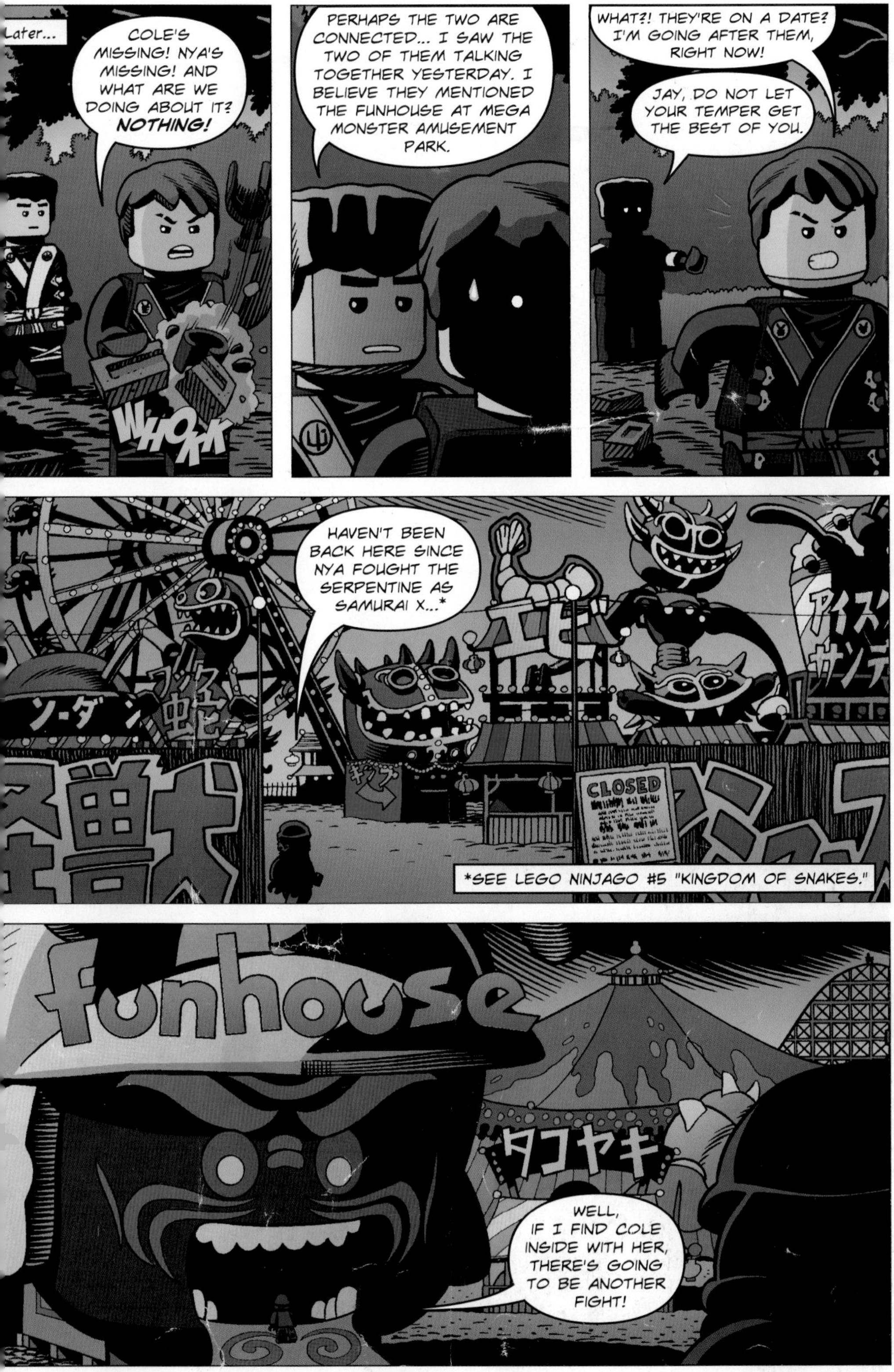

Later...
COLE'S MISSING! NYA'S MISSING! AND WHAT ARE WE DOING ABOUT IT? **NOTHING!**
PERHAPS THE TWO ARE CONNECTED... I SAW THE TWO OF THEM TALKING TOGETHER YESTERDAY. I BELIEVE THEY MENTIONED THE FUNHOUSE AT MEGA MONSTER AMUSEMENT PARK.
WHAT?! THEY'RE ON A DATE? I'M GOING AFTER THEM, RIGHT NOW!
JAY, DO NOT LET YOUR TEMPER GET THE BEST OF YOU.
HAVEN'T BEEN BACK HERE SINCE NYA FOUGHT THE SERPENTINE AS SAMURAI X...*
エビ
CLOSED
*SEE LEGO NINJAGO #5 "KINGDOM OF SNAKES."
funhouse
タコヤキ
WELL, IF I FIND COLE INSIDE WITH HER, THERE'S GOING TO BE ANOTHER FIGHT!

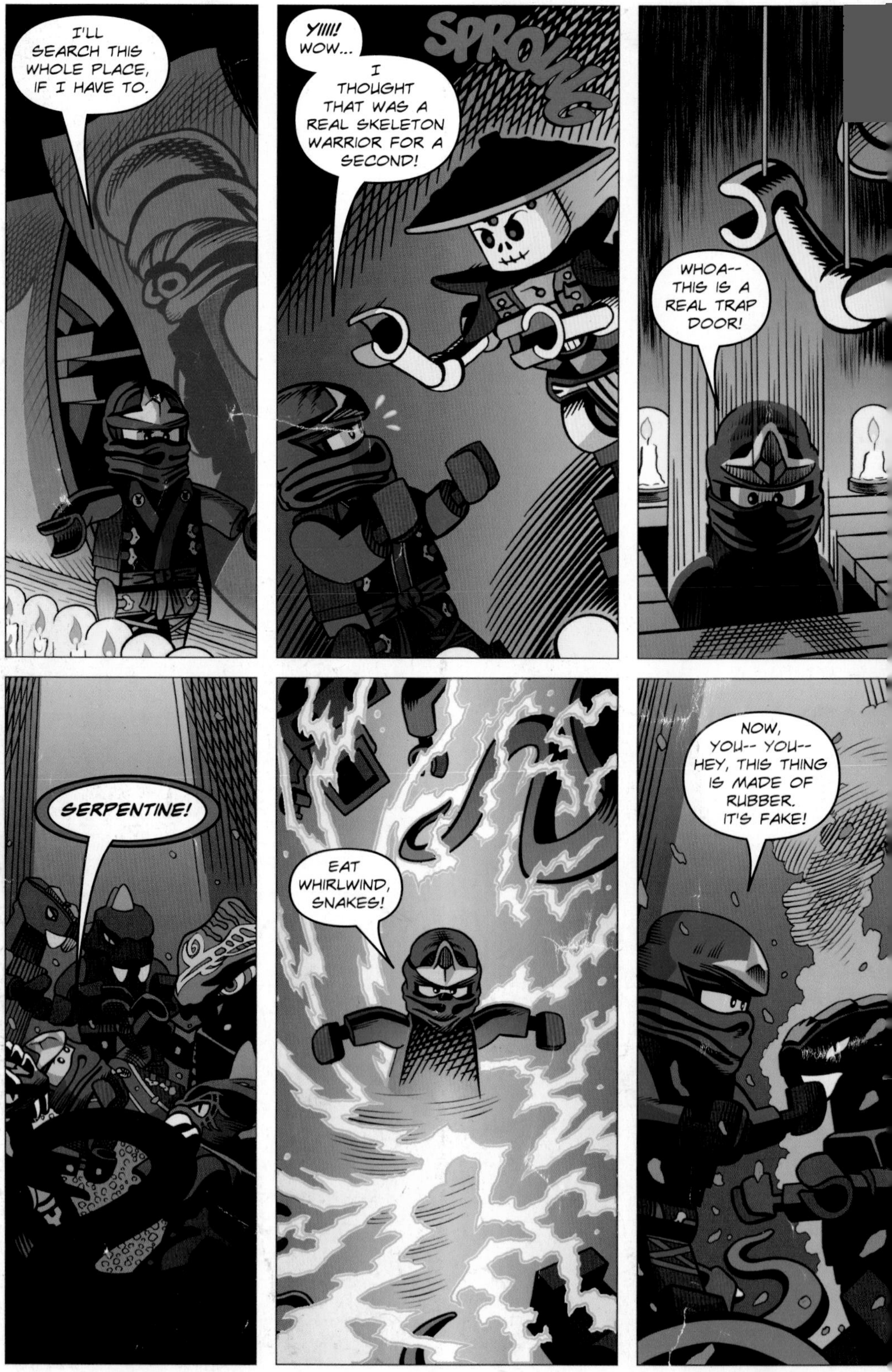
I'LL SEARCH THIS WHOLE PLACE, IF I HAVE TO.
SPROING
YIII!! WOW...
I THOUGHT THAT WAS A REAL SKELETON WARRIOR FOR A SECOND!
WHOA-- THIS IS A REAL TRAP DOOR!
SERPENTINE!
EAT WHIRLWIND, SNAKES!
NOW, YOU-- YOU-- HEY, THIS THING IS MADE OF RUBBER. IT'S FAKE!

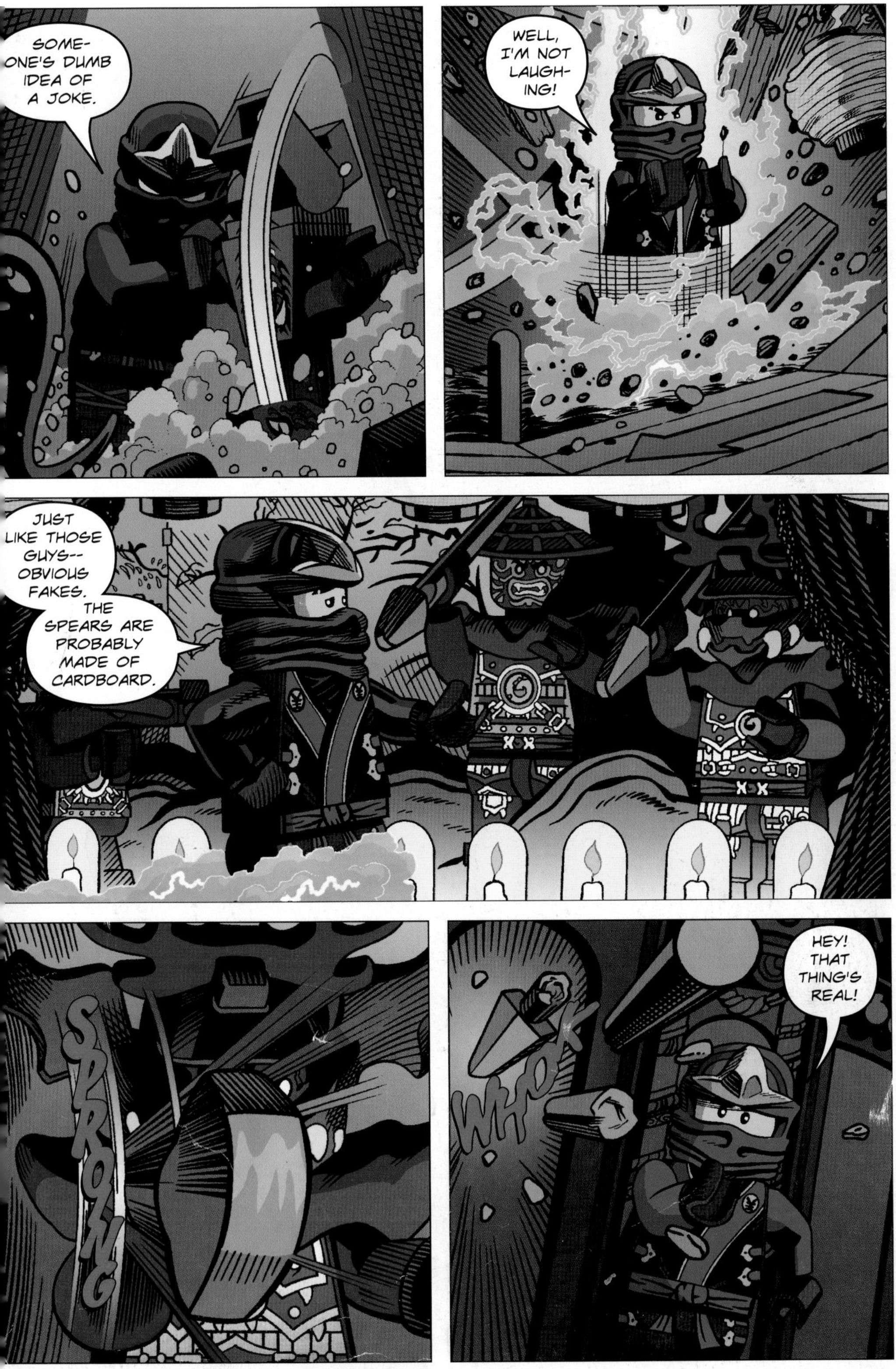
SOME-ONE'S DUMB IDEA OF A JOKE.
WELL, I'M NOT LAUGH-ING!
JUST LIKE THOSE GUYS-- OBVIOUS FAKES.
THE SPEARS ARE PROBABLY MADE OF CARDBOARD.
SPRONG
WHOK
HEY! THAT THING'S REAL!

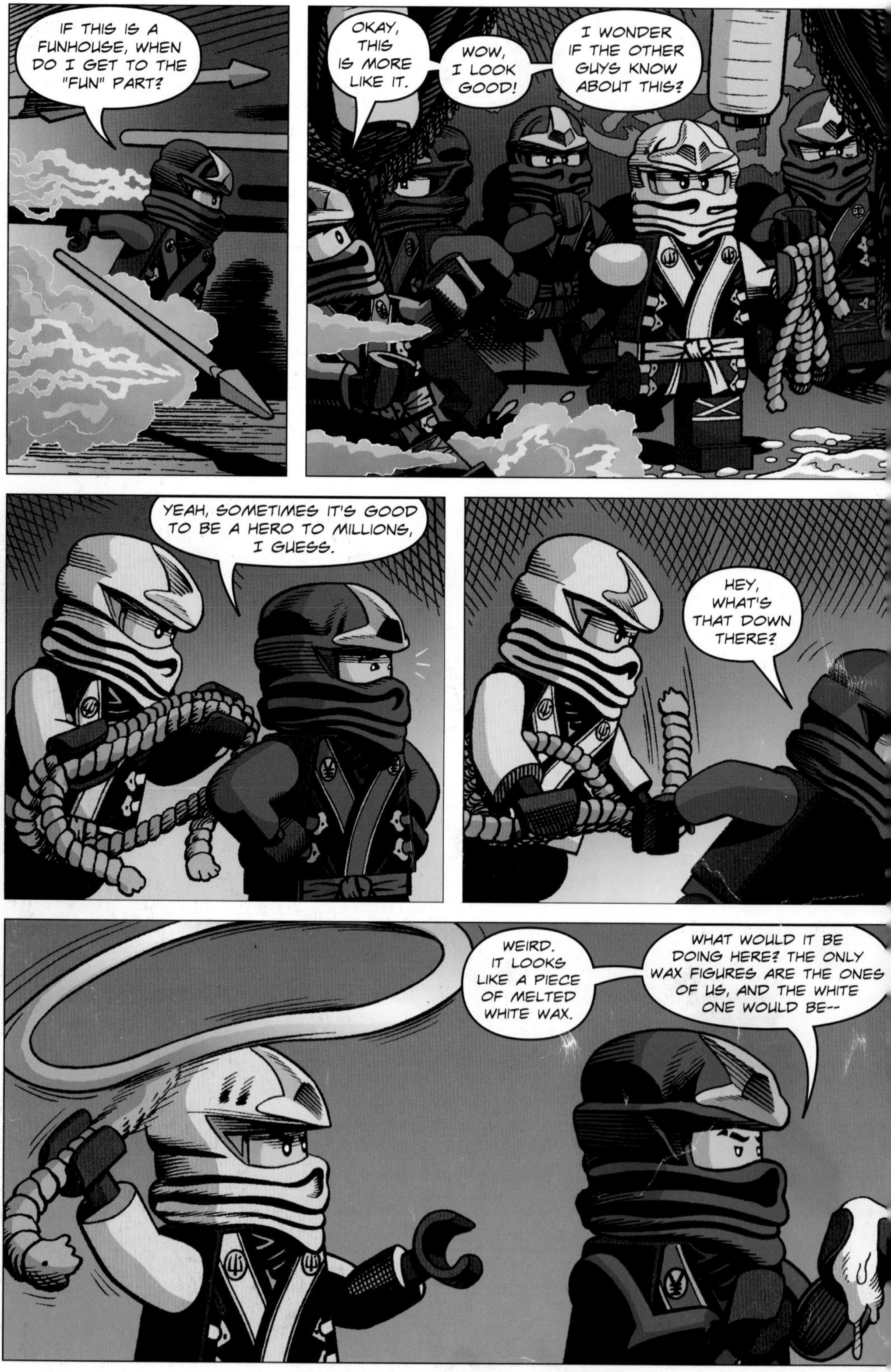
IF THIS IS A FUNHOUSE, WHEN DO I GET TO THE "FUN" PART?
OKAY, THIS IS MORE LIKE IT.
WOW, I LOOK GOOD!
I WONDER IF THE OTHER GUYS KNOW ABOUT THIS?
YEAH, SOMETIMES IT'S GOOD TO BE A HERO TO MILLIONS, I GUESS.
HEY, WHAT'S THAT DOWN THERE?
WEIRD. IT LOOKS LIKE A PIECE OF MELTED WHITE WAX.
WHAT WOULD IT BE DOING HERE? THE ONLY WAX FIGURES ARE THE ONES OF US, AND THE WHITE ONE WOULD BE--

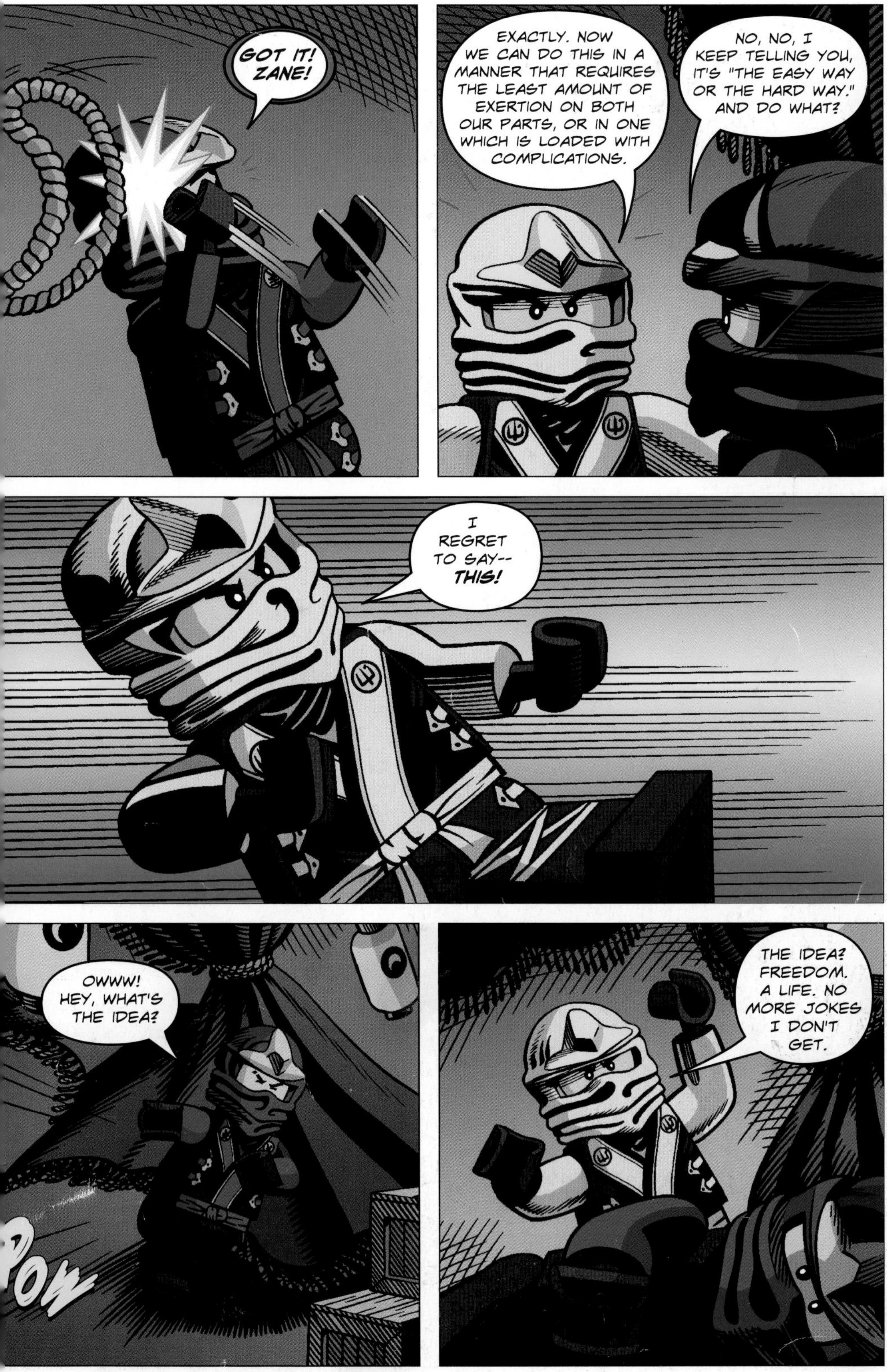
GOT IT! ZANE!
EXACTLY. NOW WE CAN DO THIS IN A MANNER THAT REQUIRES THE LEAST AMOUNT OF EXERTION ON BOTH OUR PARTS, OR IN ONE WHICH IS LOADED WITH COMPLICATIONS.
NO, NO, I KEEP TELLING YOU, IT'S "THE EASY WAY OR THE HARD WAY." AND DO WHAT?
I REGRET TO SAY-- THIS!
OWWW! HEY, WHAT'S THE IDEA?
POW
THE IDEA? FREEDOM. A LIFE. NO MORE JOKES I DON'T GET.

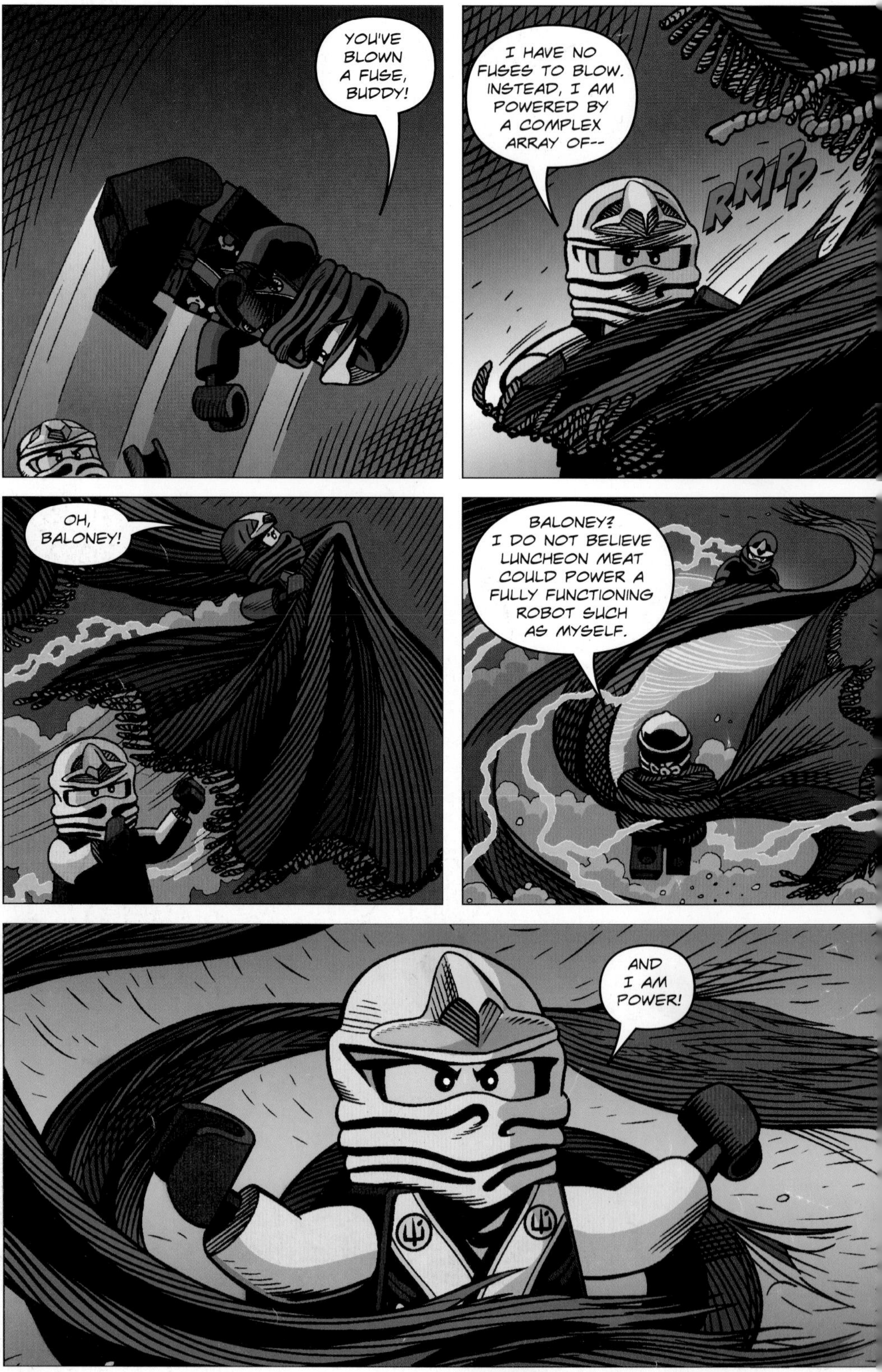
YOU'VE BLOWN A FUSE, BUDDY!
I HAVE NO FUSES TO BLOW. INSTEAD, I AM POWERED BY A COMPLEX ARRAY OF--
RRIPP
OH, BALONEY!
BALONEY? I DO NOT BELIEVE LUNCHEON MEAT COULD POWER A FULLY FUNCTIONING ROBOT SUCH AS MYSELF.
AND I AM POWER!

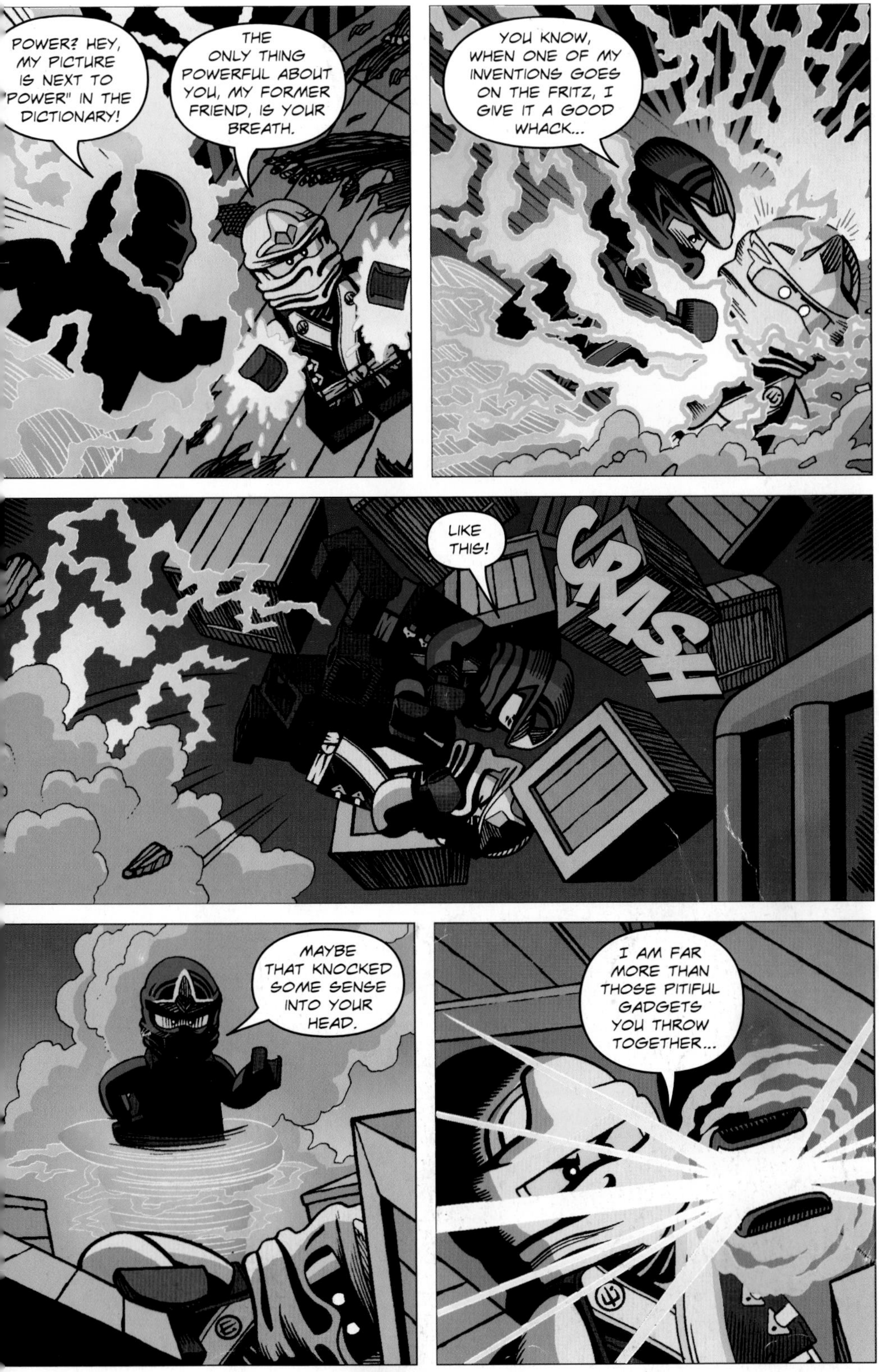
POWER? HEY, MY PICTURE IS NEXT TO "POWER" IN THE DICTIONARY!
THE ONLY THING POWERFUL ABOUT YOU, MY FORMER FRIEND, IS YOUR BREATH.
YOU KNOW, WHEN ONE OF MY INVENTIONS GOES ON THE FRITZ, I GIVE IT A GOOD WHACK...
LIKE THIS!
CRASH
MAYBE THAT KNOCKED SOME SENSE INTO YOUR HEAD.
I AM FAR MORE THAN THOSE PITIFUL GADGETS YOU THROW TOGETHER...

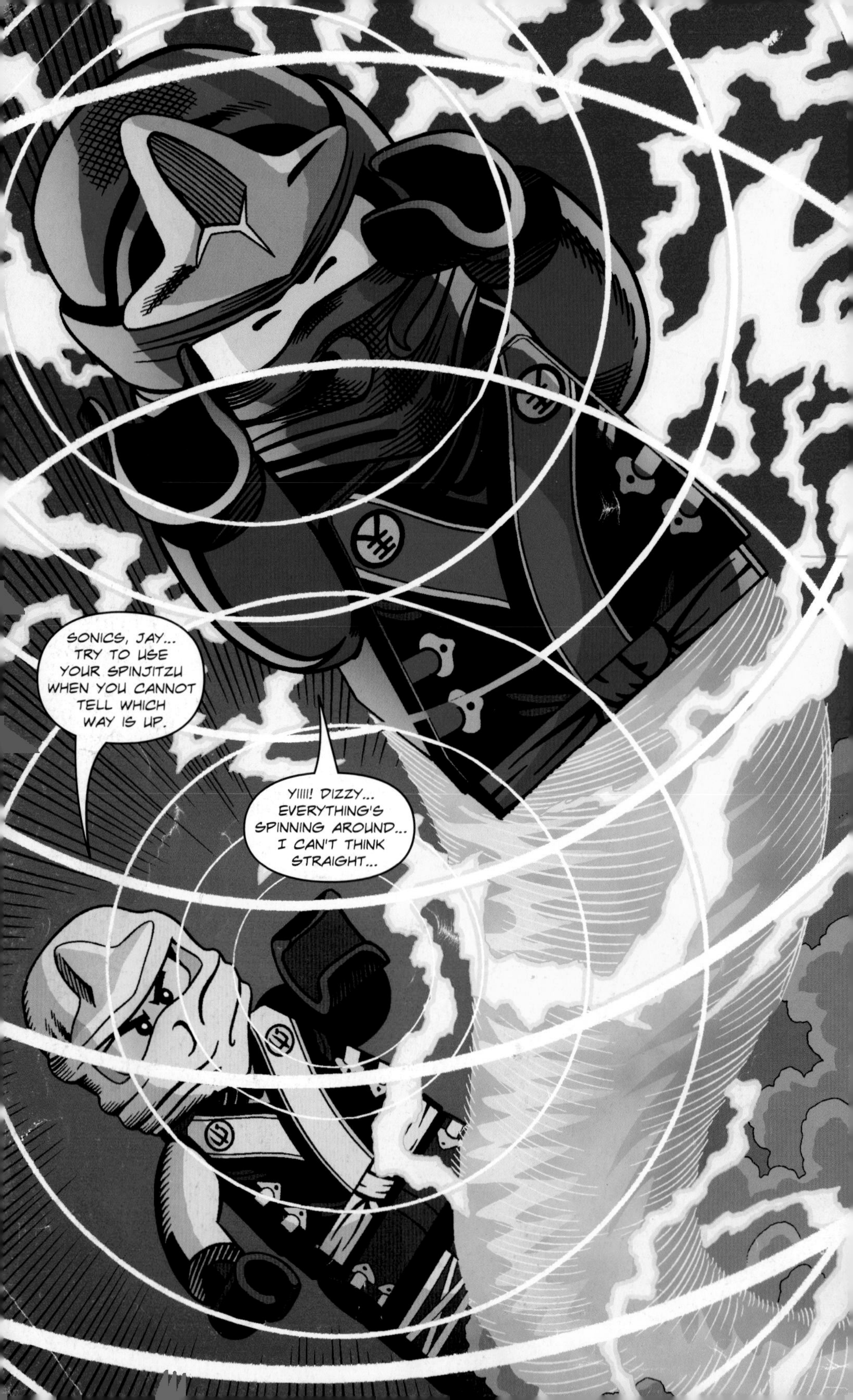
SONICS, JAY... TRY TO USE YOUR SPINJITZU WHEN YOU CANNOT TELL WHICH WAY IS UP.
YIIII! DIZZY... EVERYTHING'S SPINNING AROUND... I CAN'T THINK STRAIGHT...

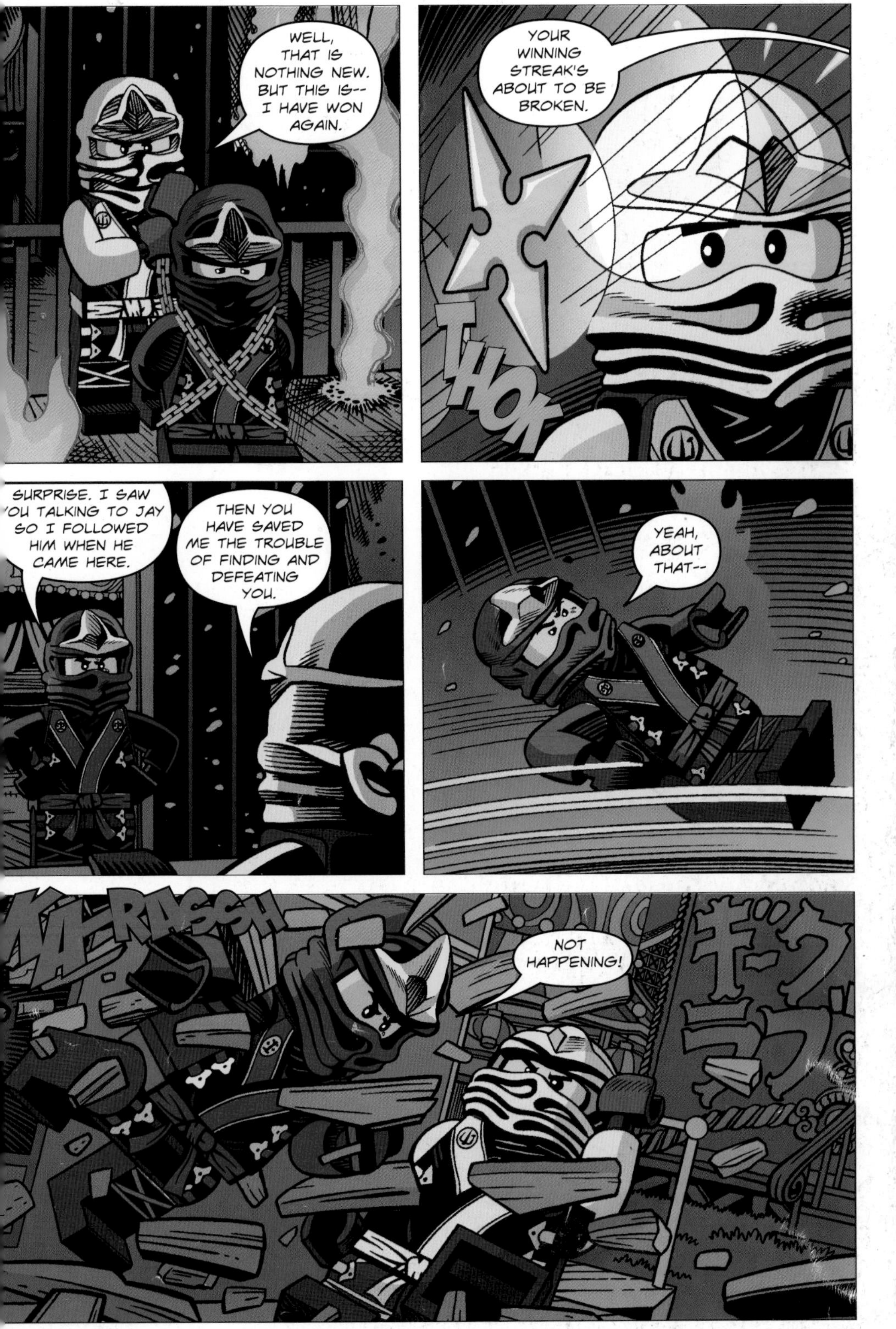
WELL, THAT IS NOTHING NEW. BUT THIS IS-- I HAVE WON AGAIN.
YOUR WINNING STREAK'S ABOUT TO BE BROKEN.
THOK
SURPRISE. I SAW YOU TALKING TO JAY SO I FOLLOWED HIM WHEN HE CAME HERE.
THEN YOU HAVE SAVED ME THE TROUBLE OF FINDING AND DEFEATING YOU.
YEAH, ABOUT THAT--
KA-RASSH
NOT HAPPENING!

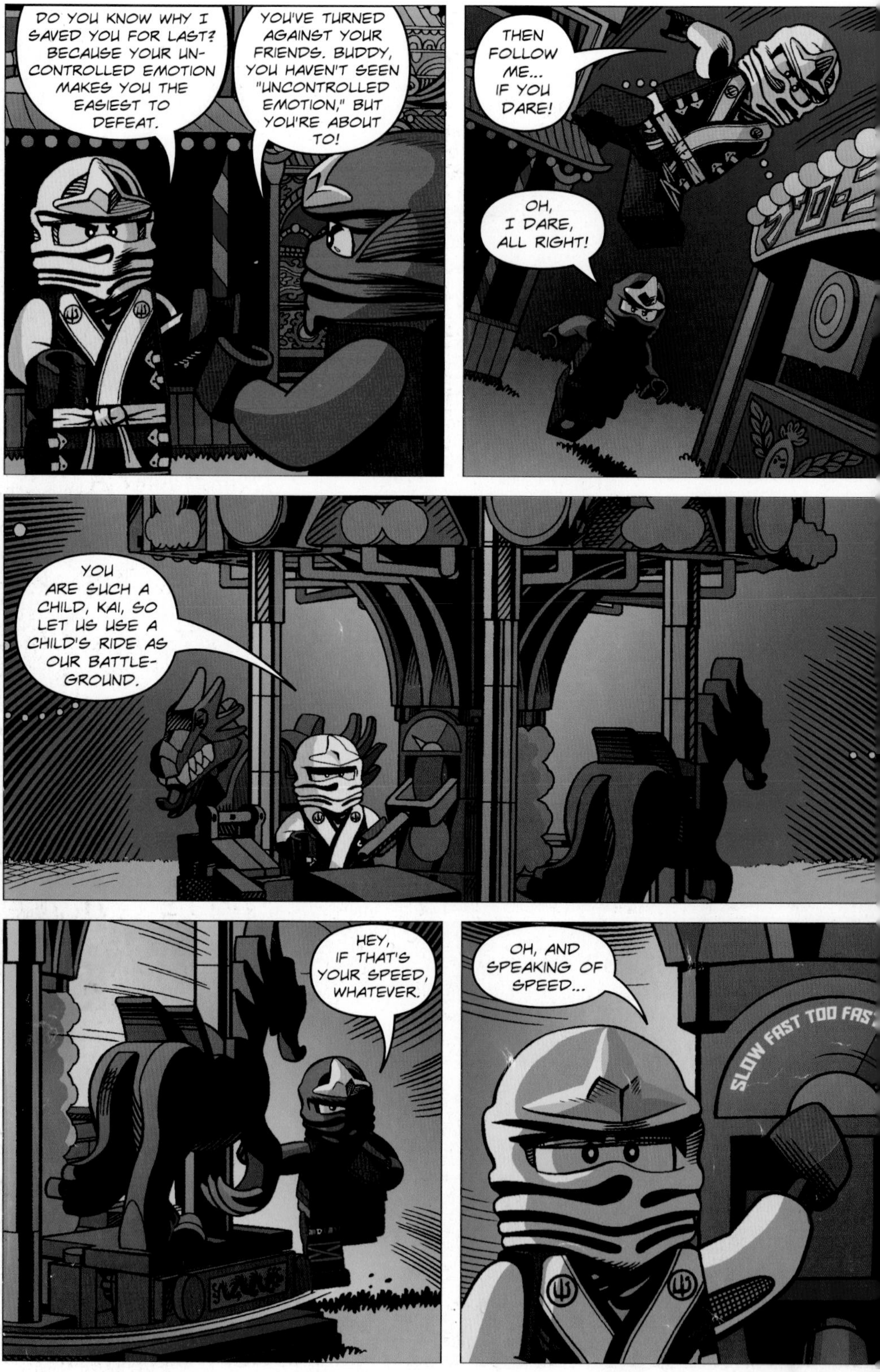
DO YOU KNOW WHY I SAVED YOU FOR LAST? BECAUSE YOUR UN-CONTROLLED EMOTION MAKES YOU THE EASIEST TO DEFEAT.
YOU'VE TURNED AGAINST YOUR FRIENDS. BUDDY, YOU HAVEN'T SEEN "UNCONTROLLED EMOTION," BUT YOU'RE ABOUT TO!
THEN FOLLOW ME... IF YOU DARE!
OH, I DARE, ALL RIGHT!
YOU ARE SUCH A CHILD, KAI, SO LET US USE A CHILD'S RIDE AS OUR BATTLE-GROUND.
HEY, IF THAT'S YOUR SPEED, WHATEVER.
OH, AND SPEAKING OF SPEED...
SLOW FAST TOO FAS

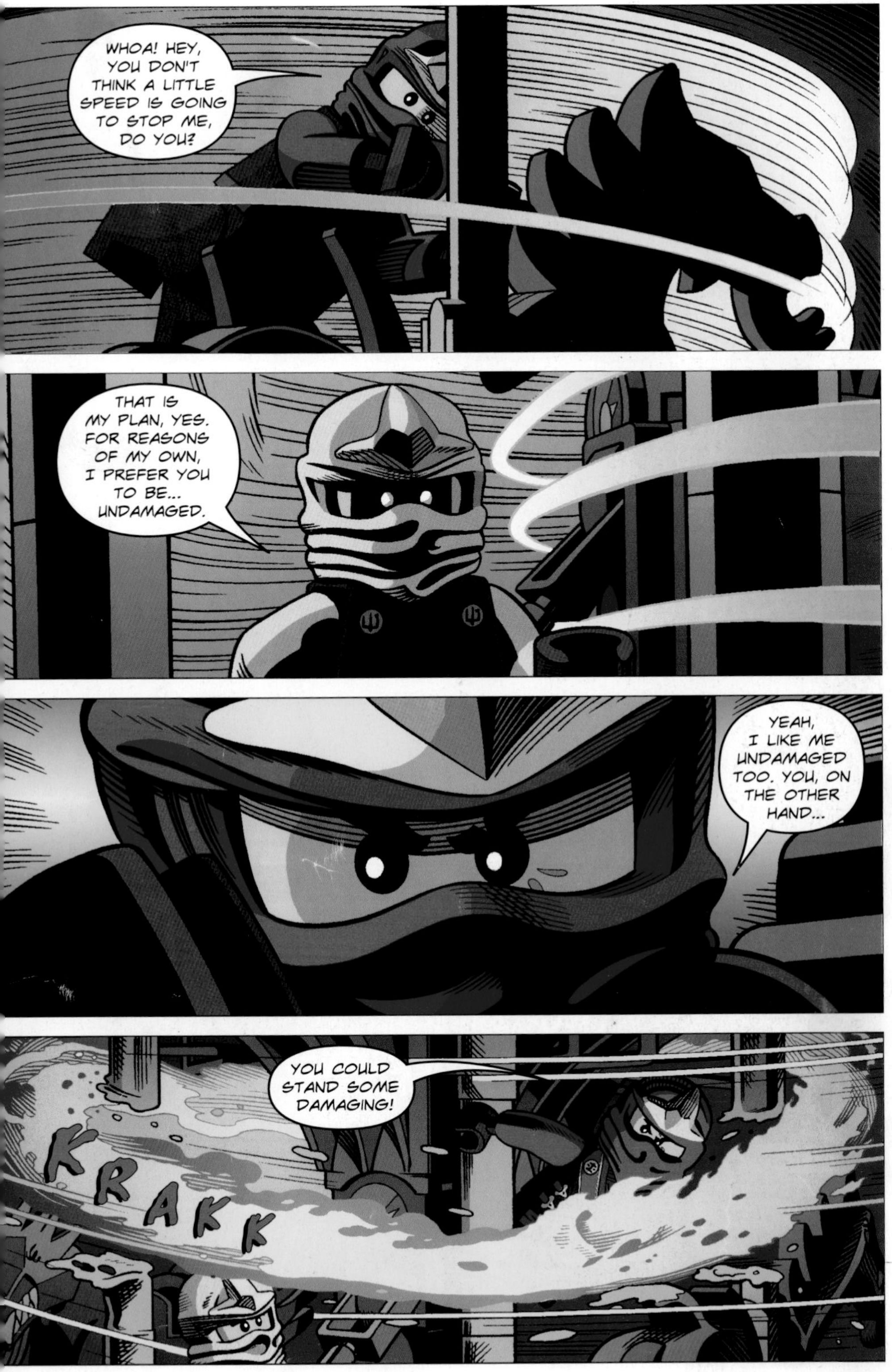
WHOA! HEY, YOU DON'T THINK A LITTLE SPEED IS GOING TO STOP ME, DO YOU?
THAT IS MY PLAN, YES. FOR REASONS OF MY OWN, I PREFER YOU TO BE... UNDAMAGED.
YEAH, I LIKE ME UNDAMAGED TOO. YOU, ON THE OTHER HAND...
YOU COULD STAND SOME DAMAGING!
KRAKK

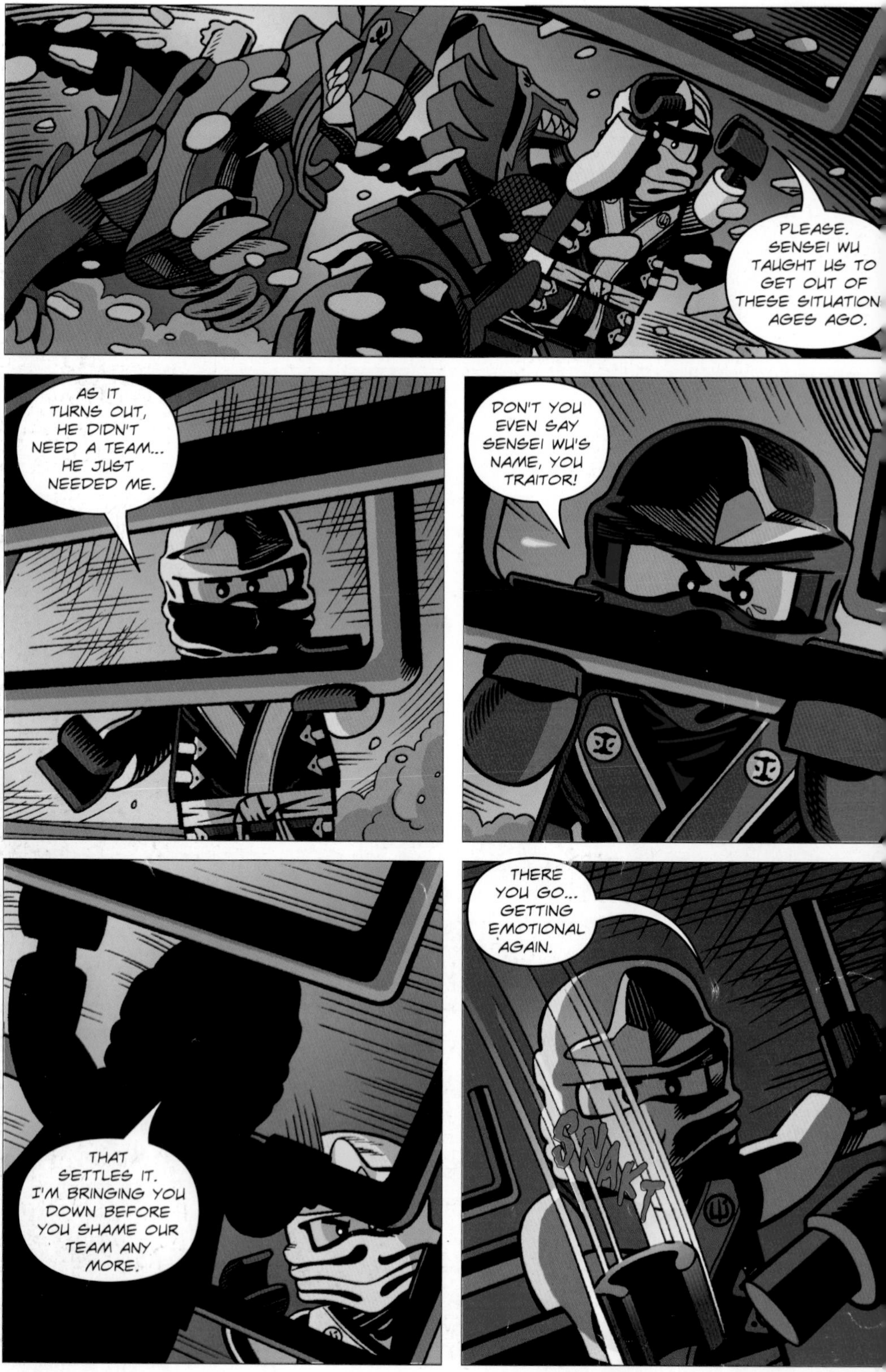
PLEASE. SENSEI WU TAUGHT US TO GET OUT OF THESE SITUATION AGES AGO.
AS IT TURNS OUT, HE DIDN'T NEED A TEAM... HE JUST NEEDED ME.
DON'T YOU EVEN SAY SENSEI WU'S NAME, YOU TRAITOR!
THAT SETTLES IT. I'M BRINGING YOU DOWN BEFORE YOU SHAME OUR TEAM ANY MORE.
THERE YOU GO... GETTING EMOTIONAL AGAIN.
SNAKT

PRETTY GOOD, ZANE. BUT YOU KNOW WHAT?

NOT --

GOOD--

ENOUGH!

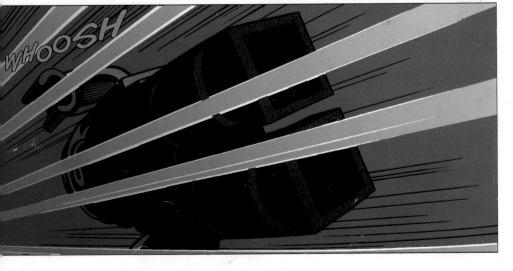

WHOOSH

39

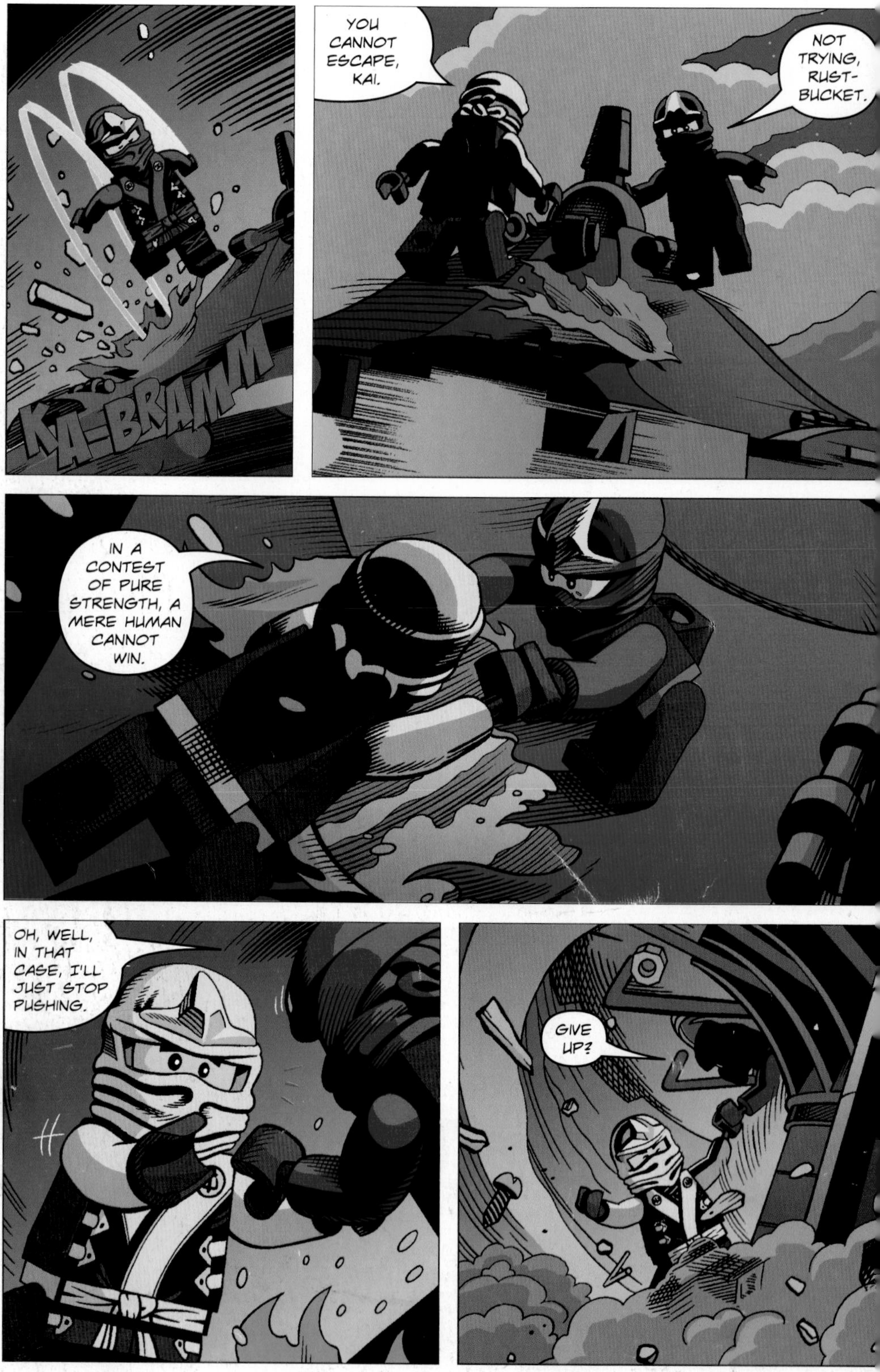
KA-BRAMM
YOU CANNOT ESCAPE, KAI.
NOT TRYING, RUST-BUCKET.
IN A CONTEST OF PURE STRENGTH, A MERE HUMAN CANNOT WIN.
OH, WELL, IN THAT CASE, I'LL JUST STOP PUSHING.
GIVE UP?

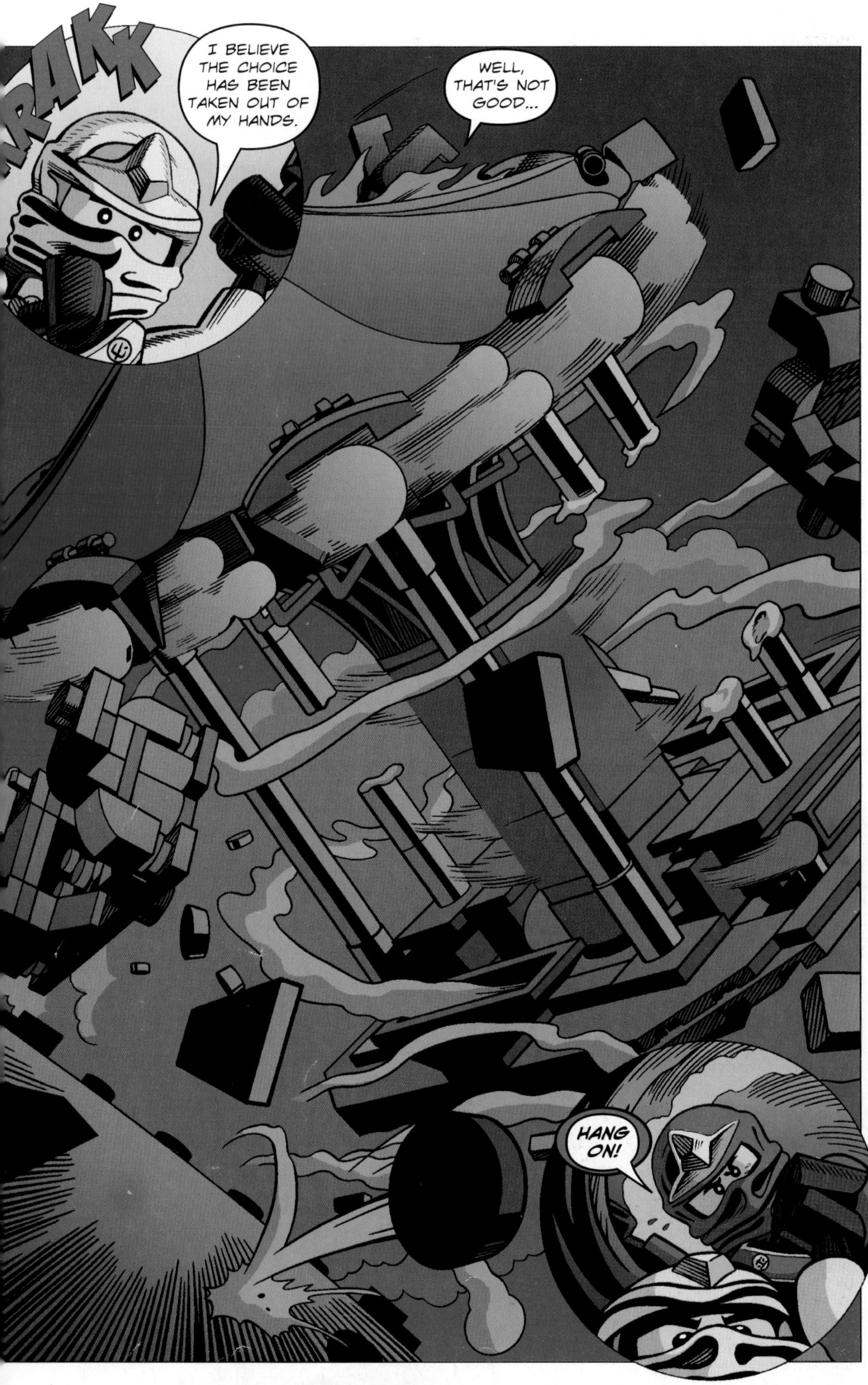
KRAKK
I BELIEVE THE CHOICE HAS BEEN TAKEN OUT OF MY HANDS.
WELL, THAT'S NOT GOOD...
HANG ON!

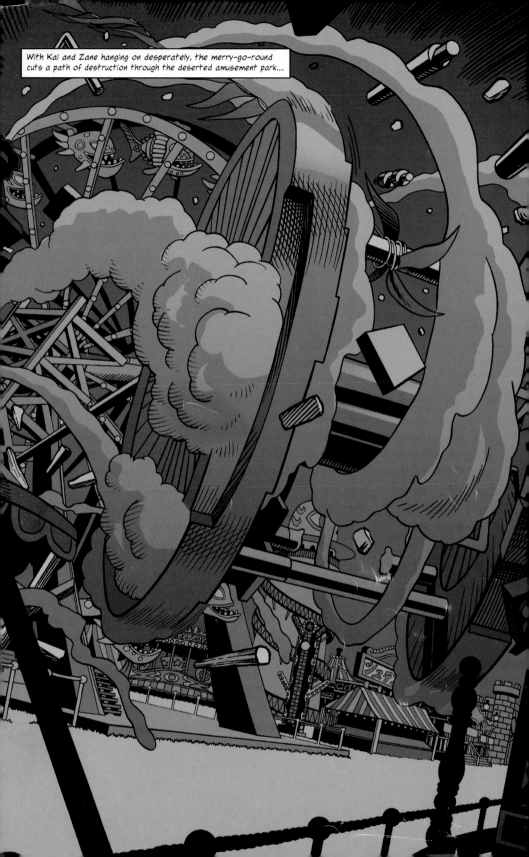

With Kai and Zane hanging on desperately, the merry-go-round cuts a path of destruction through the deserted amusement park...

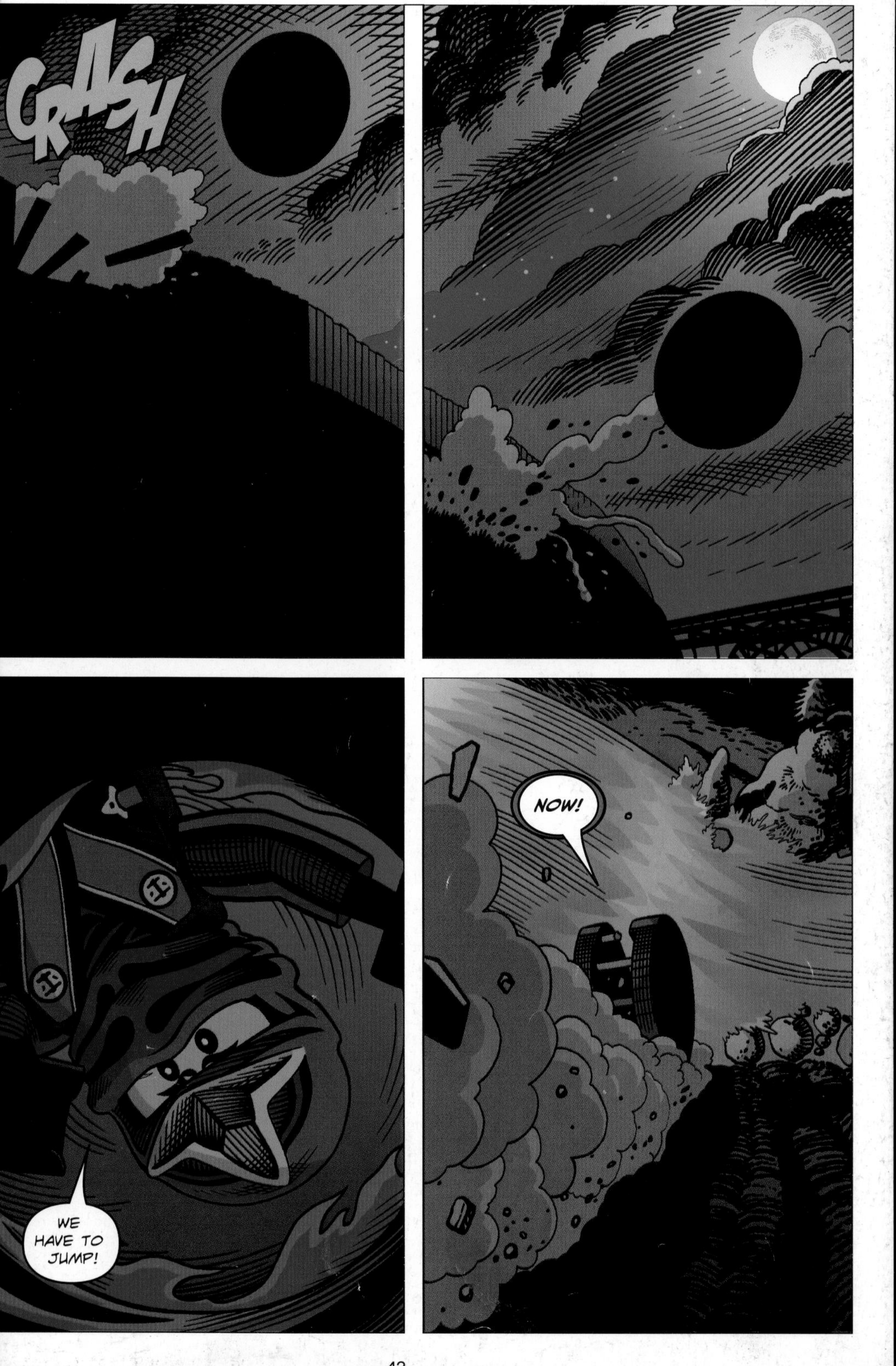
CRASH
WE HAVE TO JUMP!
NOW!

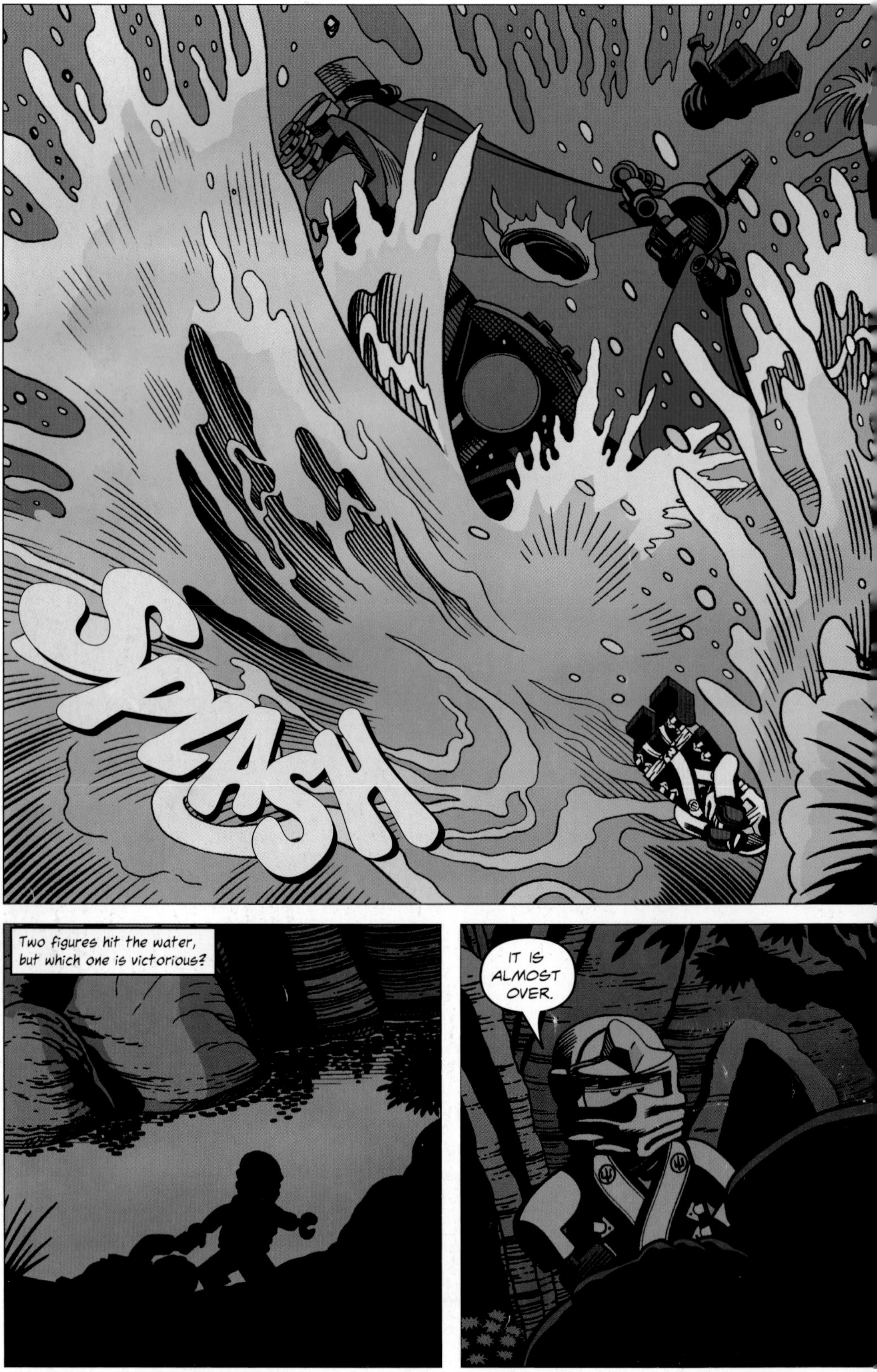
SPLASH
Two figures hit the water, but which one is victorious?
IT IS ALMOST OVER.

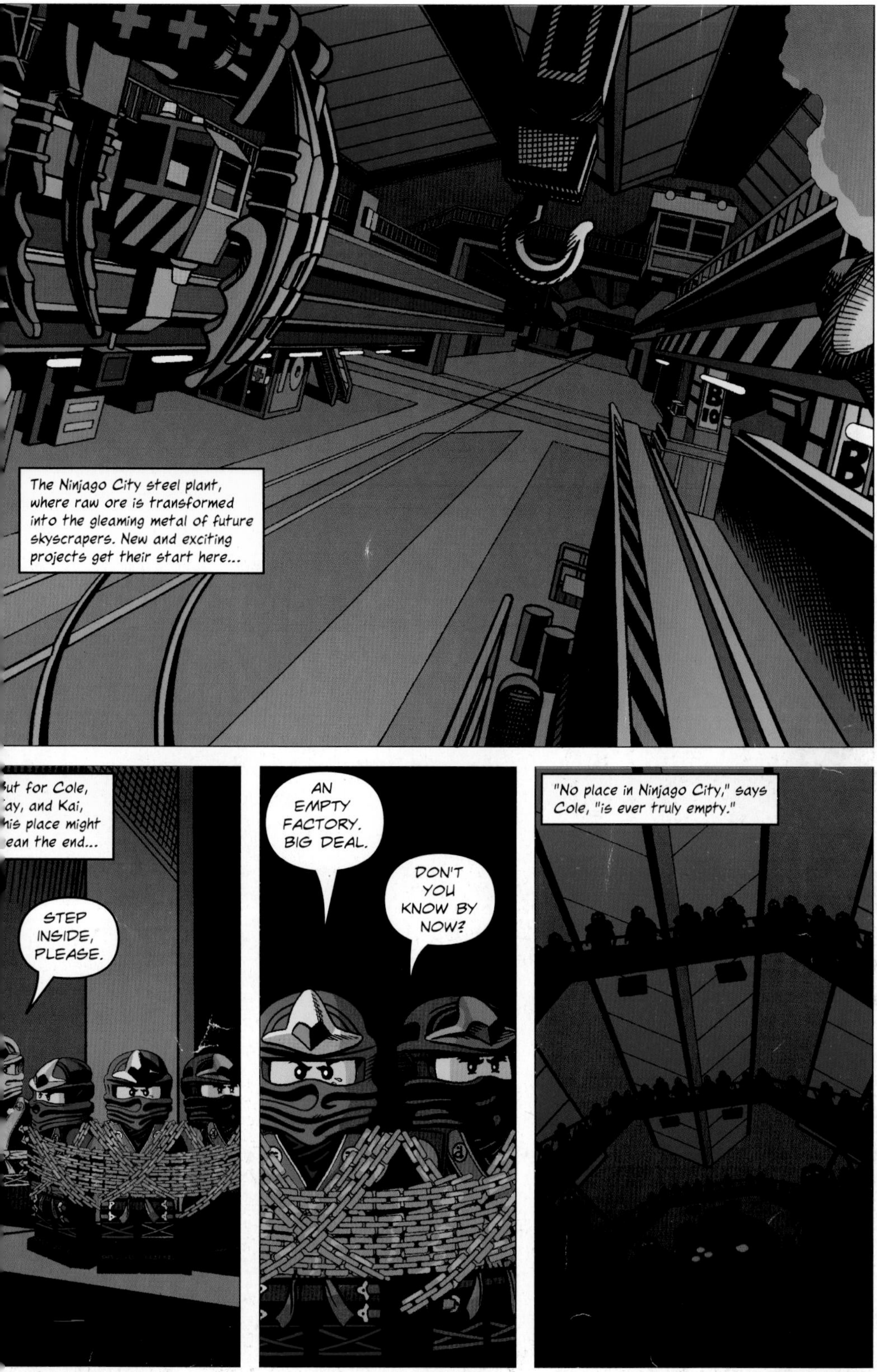
The Ninjago City steel plant, where raw ore is transformed into the gleaming metal of future skyscrapers. New and exciting projects get their start here...
ut for Cole, ay, and Kai, his place might ean the end...
STEP INSIDE, PLEASE.
AN EMPTY FACTORY. BIG DEAL.
DON'T YOU KNOW BY NOW?
"No place in Ninjago City," says Cole, "is ever truly empty."

OVERLORD! I'VE KEPT MY PART OF THE BARGAIN! NOW KEEP YOURS!

YOU ROTTEN TRAITOR! LET ME OUT OF THESE CHAINS AND I'LL--

AH, BUT YOU WON'T BE ESCAPING YOUR CHAINS, NINJA... NOT NOW, NOT EVER.

WHERE IS HE?

THERE ARE SPEAKERS WIRED TO THE CAT-WALKS.

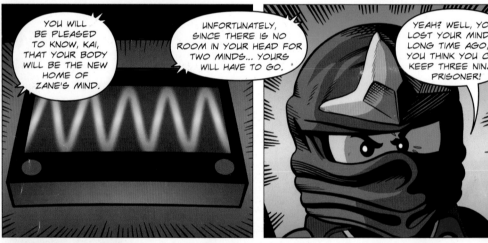

YOU WILL BE PLEASED TO KNOW, KAI, THAT YOUR BODY WILL BE THE NEW HOME OF ZANE'S MIND.

UNFORTUNATELY, SINCE THERE IS NO ROOM IN YOUR HEAD FOR TWO MINDS... YOURS WILL HAVE TO GO.

YEAH? WELL, YOU LOST YOUR MIND A LONG TIME AGO, IF YOU THINK YOU CAN KEEP THREE NINJA PRISONER!

PRISONERS? NO, YOU ARE FAR TOO... ANNOYING FOR THAT. I HAVE OTHER PLANS.

46

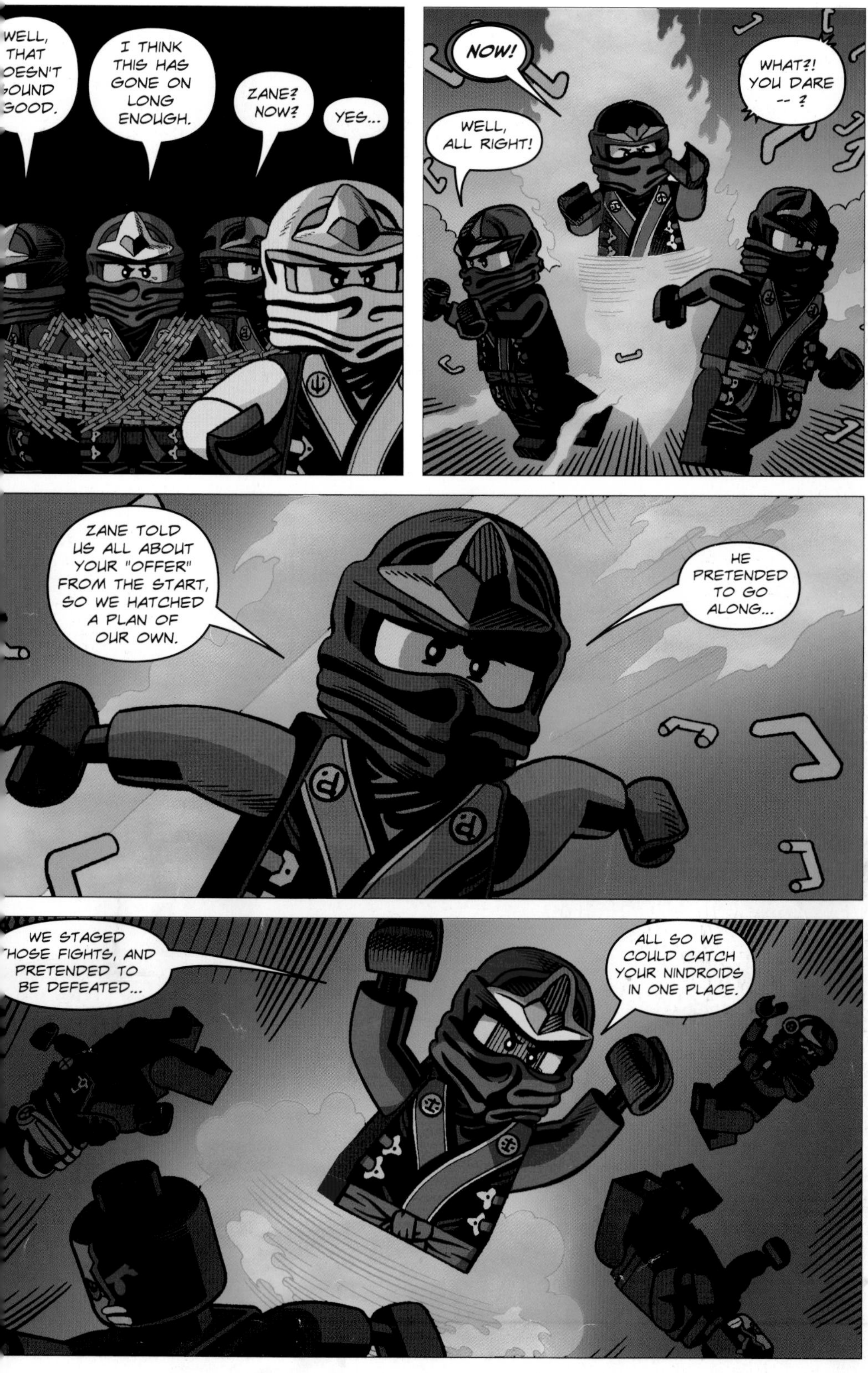
WELL, THAT OESN'T OUND GOOD.
I THINK THIS HAS GONE ON LONG ENOUGH.
ZANE? NOW?
YES...
NOW!
WELL, ALL RIGHT!
WHAT?! YOU DARE -- ?
ZANE TOLD US ALL ABOUT YOUR "OFFER" FROM THE START, SO WE HATCHED A PLAN OF OUR OWN.
HE PRETENDED TO GO ALONG...
WE STAGED HOSE FIGHTS, AND PRETENDED TO BE DEFEATED...
ALL SO WE COULD CATCH YOUR NINDROIDS IN ONE PLACE.

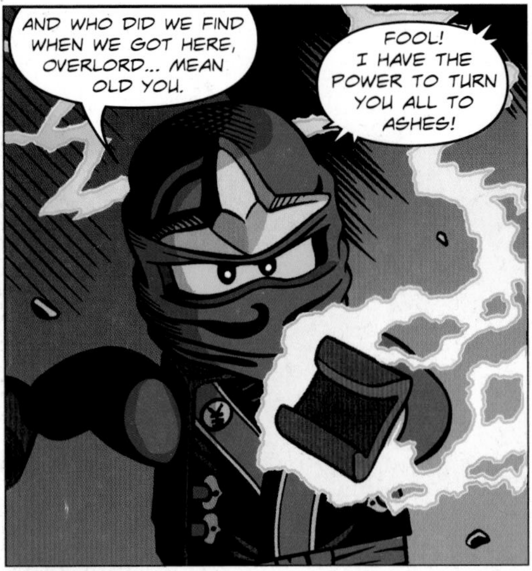
AND WHO DID WE FIND WHEN WE GOT HERE, OVERLORD... MEAN OLD YOU.
FOOL! I HAVE THE POWER TO TURN YOU ALL TO ASHES!

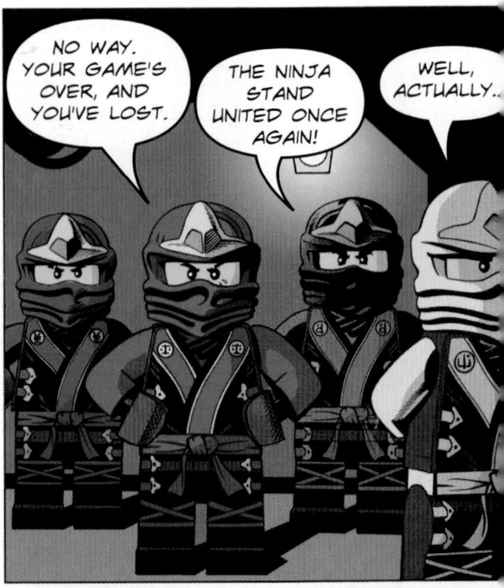
NO WAY. YOUR GAME'S OVER, AND YOU'VE LOST.
THE NINJA STAND UNITED ONCE AGAIN!
WELL, ACTUALLY...

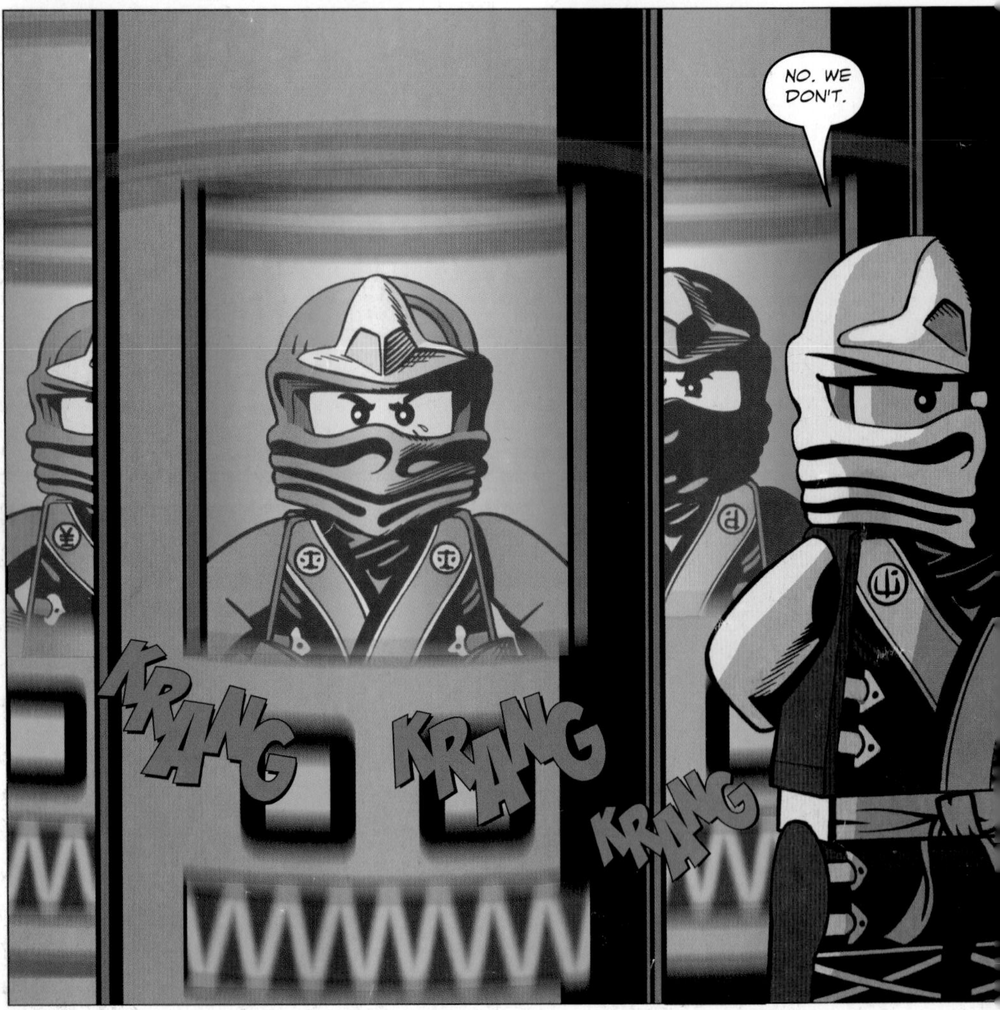
NO. WE DON'T.
KRANG
KRANG
KRANG

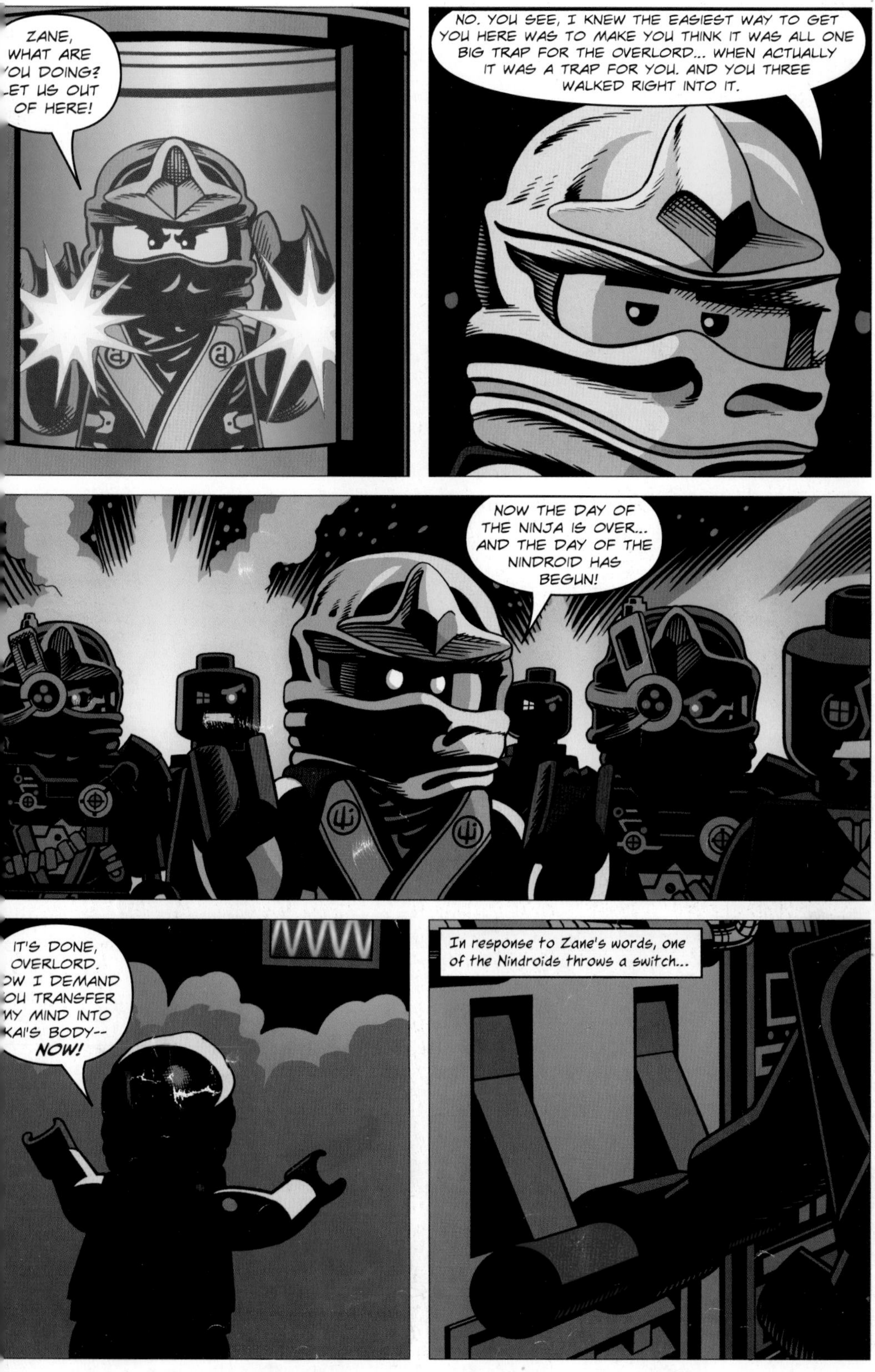
ZANE, WHAT ARE 'OU DOING? ET US OUT OF HERE!
NO. YOU SEE, I KNEW THE EASIEST WAY TO GET YOU HERE WAS TO MAKE YOU THINK IT WAS ALL ONE BIG TRAP FOR THE OVERLORD... WHEN ACTUALLY IT WAS A TRAP FOR YOU. AND YOU THREE WALKED RIGHT INTO IT.
NOW THE DAY OF THE NINJA IS OVER... AND THE DAY OF THE NINDROID HAS BEGUN!
IT'S DONE, OVERLORD. OW I DEMAND OU TRANSFER MY MIND INTO KAI'S BODY-- **NOW!**
In response to Zane's words, one of the Nindroids throws a switch...

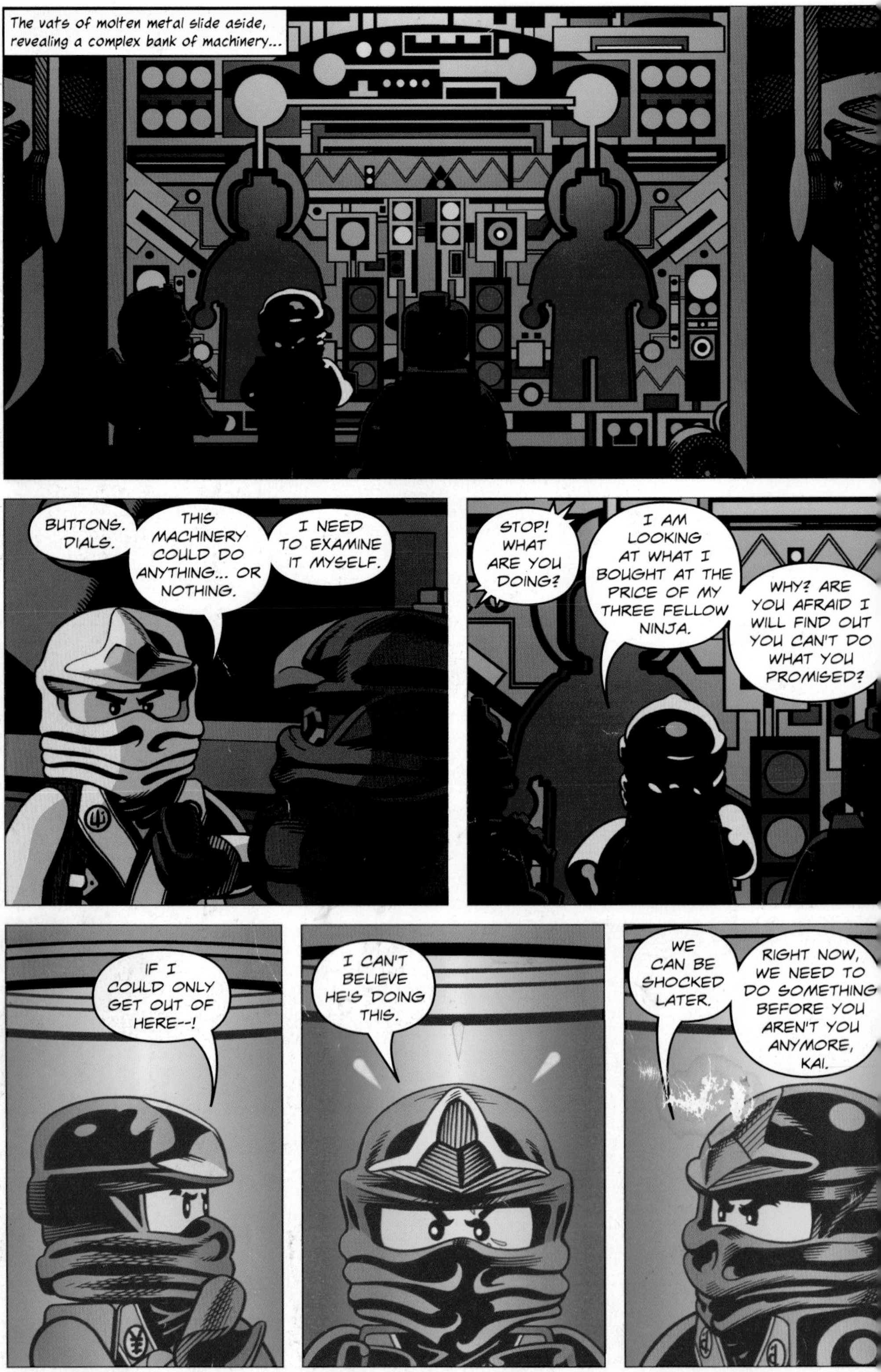

The vats of molten metal slide aside, revealing a complex bank of machinery...
BUTTONS. DIALS.
THIS MACHINERY COULD DO ANYTHING... OR NOTHING.
I NEED TO EXAMINE IT MYSELF.
STOP! WHAT ARE YOU DOING?
I AM LOOKING AT WHAT I BOUGHT AT THE PRICE OF MY THREE FELLOW NINJA.
WHY? ARE YOU AFRAID I WILL FIND OUT YOU CAN'T DO WHAT YOU PROMISED?
IF I COULD ONLY GET OUT OF HERE--!
I CAN'T BELIEVE HE'S DOING THIS.
WE CAN BE SHOCKED LATER.
RIGHT NOW, WE NEED TO DO SOMETHING BEFORE YOU AREN'T YOU ANYMORE, KAI.

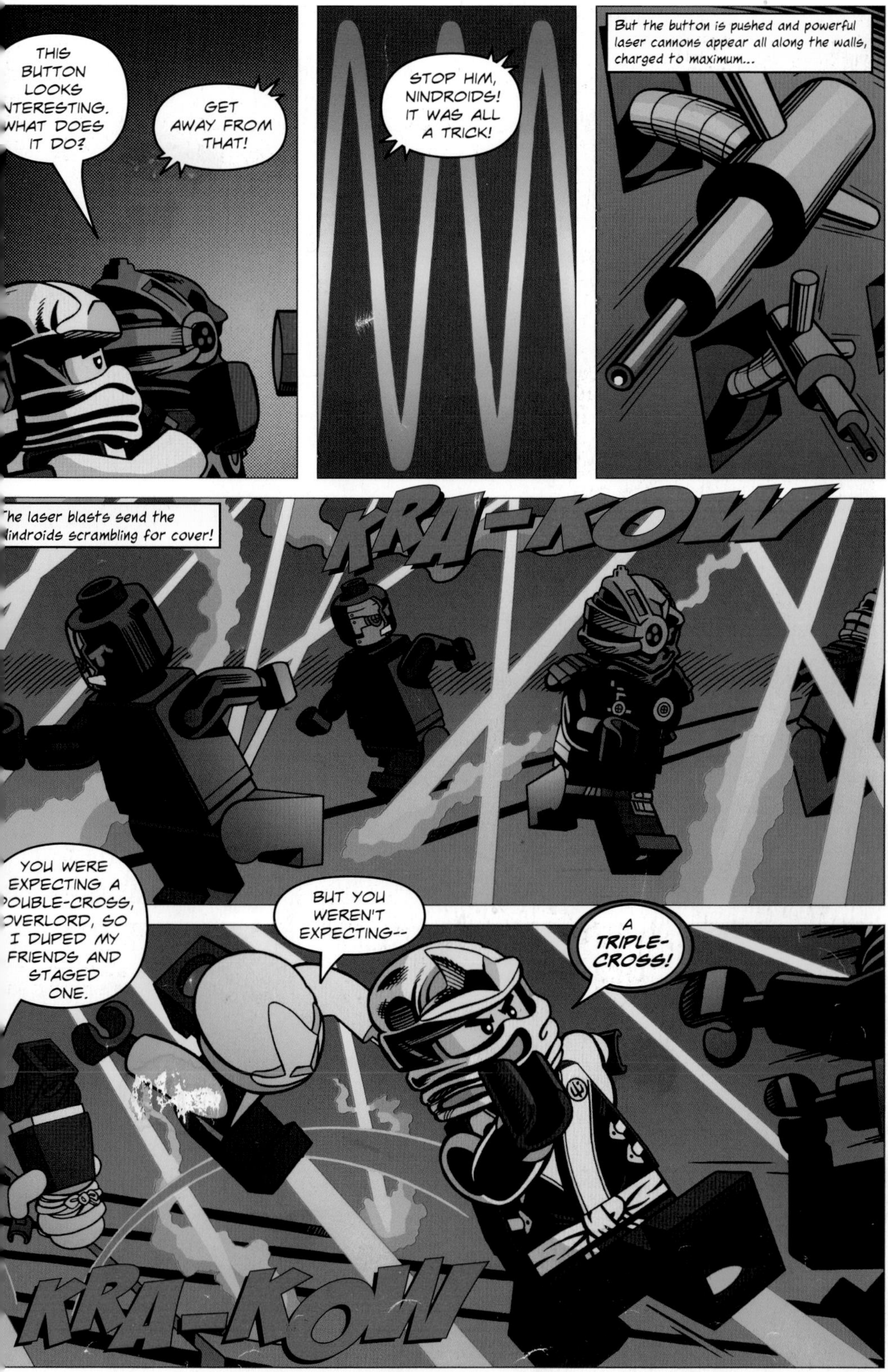

THIS BUTTON LOOKS INTERESTING. WHAT DOES IT DO?
GET AWAY FROM THAT!
STOP HIM, NINDROIDS! IT WAS ALL A TRICK!
But the button is pushed and powerful laser cannons appear all along the walls, charged to maximum...
The laser blasts send the Nindroids scrambling for cover!
KRA-KOW
YOU WERE EXPECTING A DOUBLE-CROSS, OVERLORD, SO I DUPED MY FRIENDS AND STAGED ONE.
BUT YOU WEREN'T EXPECTING--
A TRIPLE-CROSS!
KRA-KOW

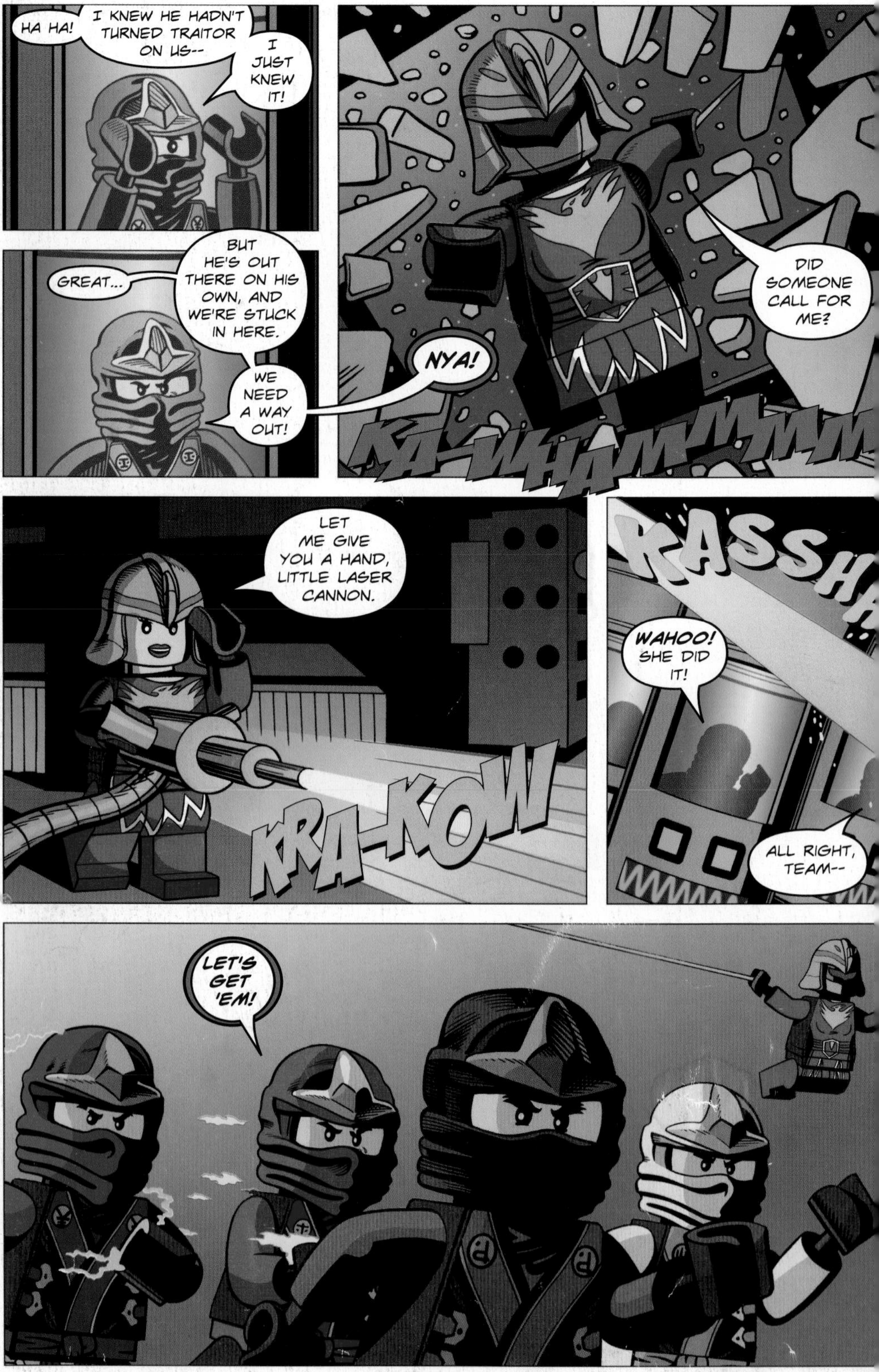
HA HA!
I KNEW HE HADN'T TURNED TRAITOR ON US--
I JUST KNEW IT!
GREAT...
BUT HE'S OUT THERE ON HIS OWN, AND WE'RE STUCK IN HERE.
WE NEED A WAY OUT!
NYA!
DID SOMEONE CALL FOR ME?
KA-WHAMMMMM
LET ME GIVE YOU A HAND, LITTLE LASER CANNON.
KRA-KOW
KASSH
WAHOO! SHE DID IT!
ALL RIGHT, TEAM--
LET'S GET 'EM!

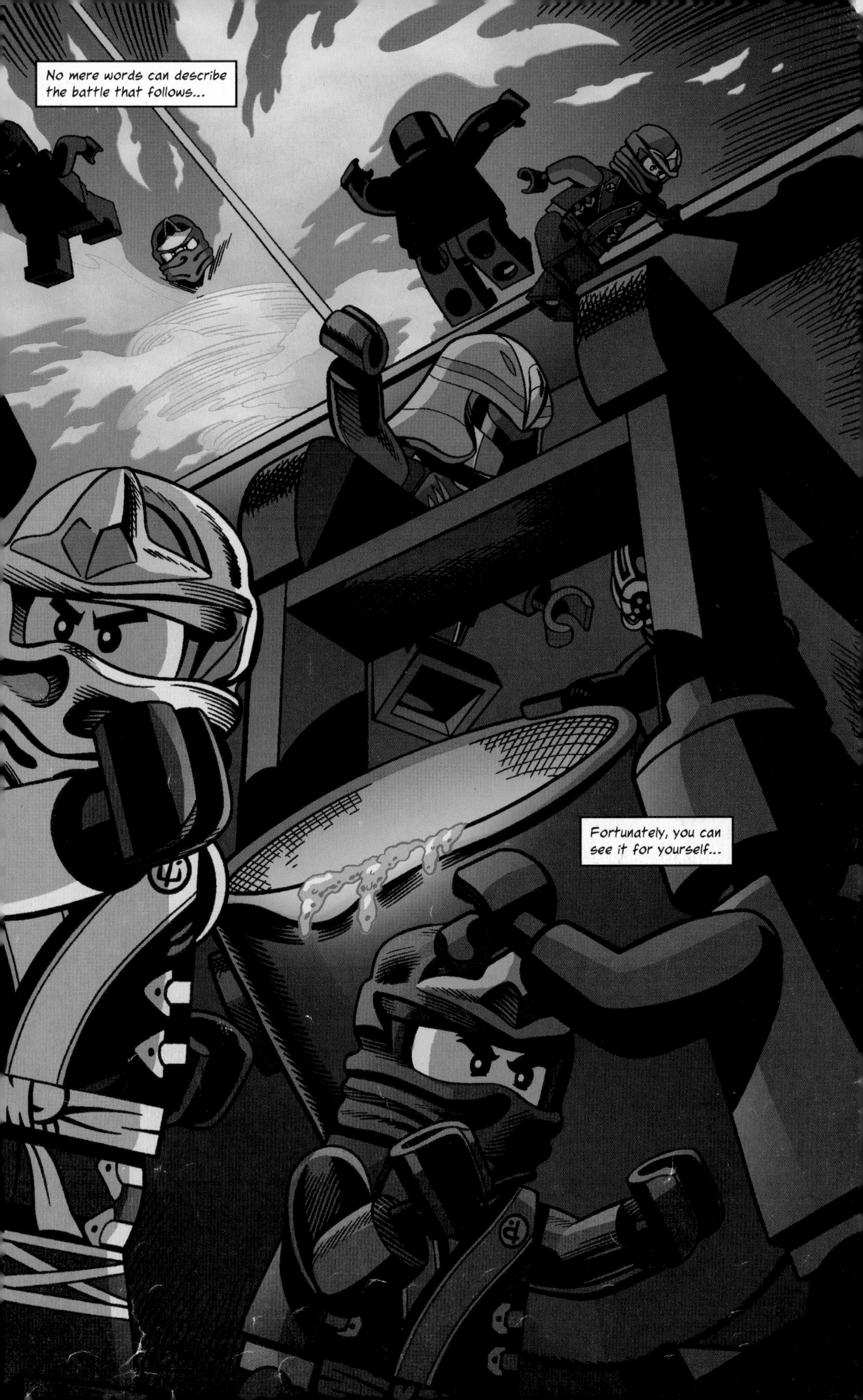
No mere words can describe the battle that follows...
Fortunately, you can see it for yourself...

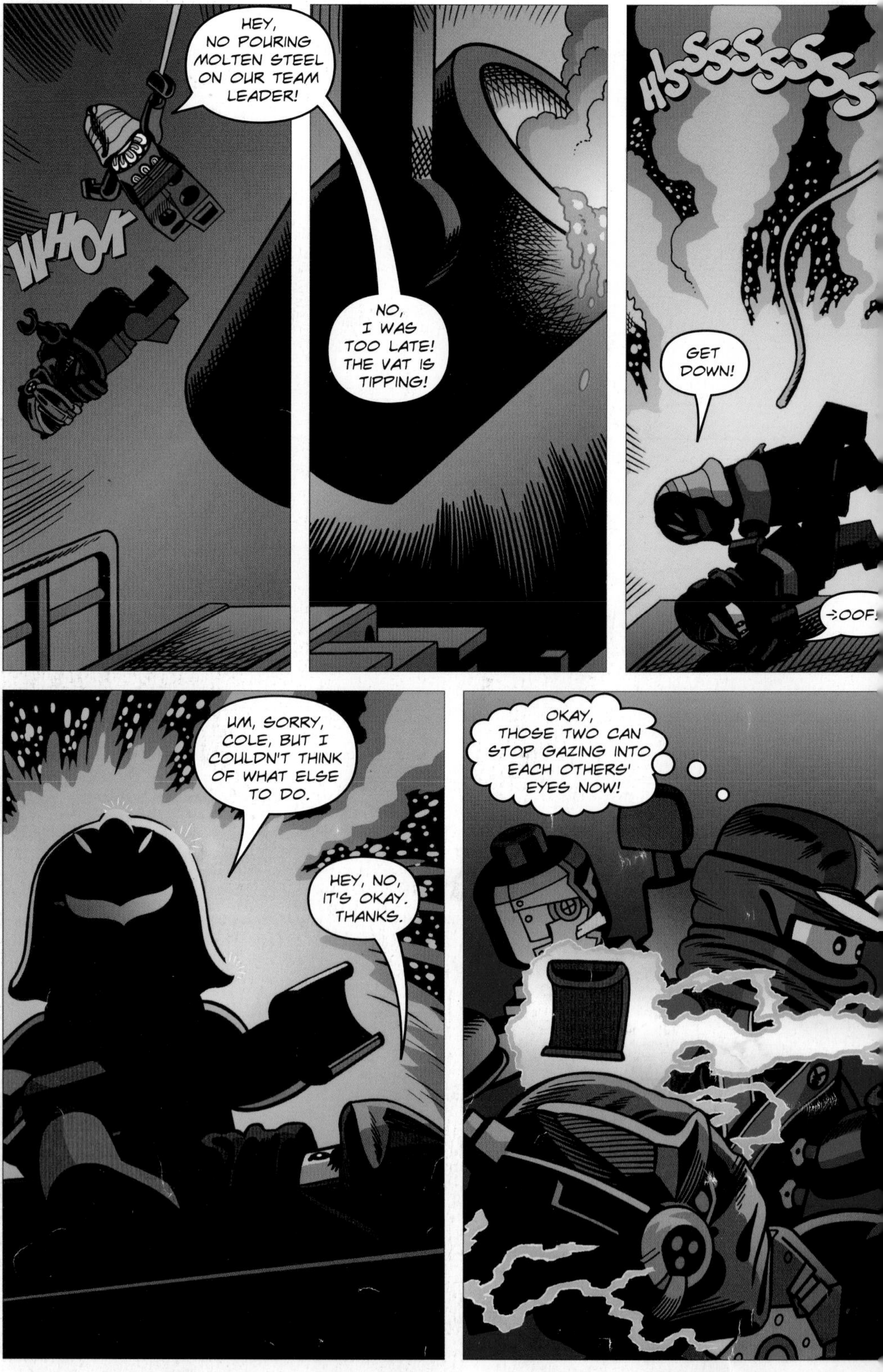
HEY, NO POURING MOLTEN STEEL ON OUR TEAM LEADER!
WHOK
NO, I WAS TOO LATE! THE VAT IS TIPPING!
HISSSSSSSSS
GET DOWN!
OOF!
UM, SORRY, COLE, BUT I COULDN'T THINK OF WHAT ELSE TO DO.
HEY, NO, IT'S OKAY. THANKS.
OKAY, THOSE TWO CAN STOP GAZING INTO EACH OTHERS' EYES NOW!

YOU'RE A FOOL, ZANE. YOU HAVE FORFEITED YOUR CHANCE AT HUMANITY.

NO. IF I HAD DONE WHAT YOU ASKED, I MIGHT HAVE HAD A HUMAN BODY... BUT I WOULD HAVE BEEN FAR FROM HUMAN.

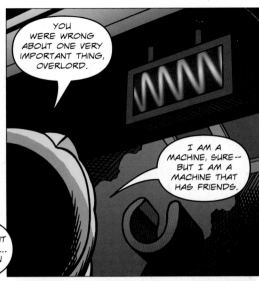

YOU WERE WRONG ABOUT ONE VERY IMPORTANT THING, OVERLORD.

I AM A MACHINE, SURE-- BUT I AM A MACHINE THAT HAS FRIENDS.

AND I WILL STAND OR FALL BESIDE THEM!

I VOTE FOR "STAND." ONE... TWO...

KZZZ AAKK

THREE!

GOOD TO KNOW YOU'VE GOT MY BACK, BUDDY.

YOUR BACK? I DO NOT HAVE YOUR BACK. IT IS STILL WHERE IT ALWAYS IS.

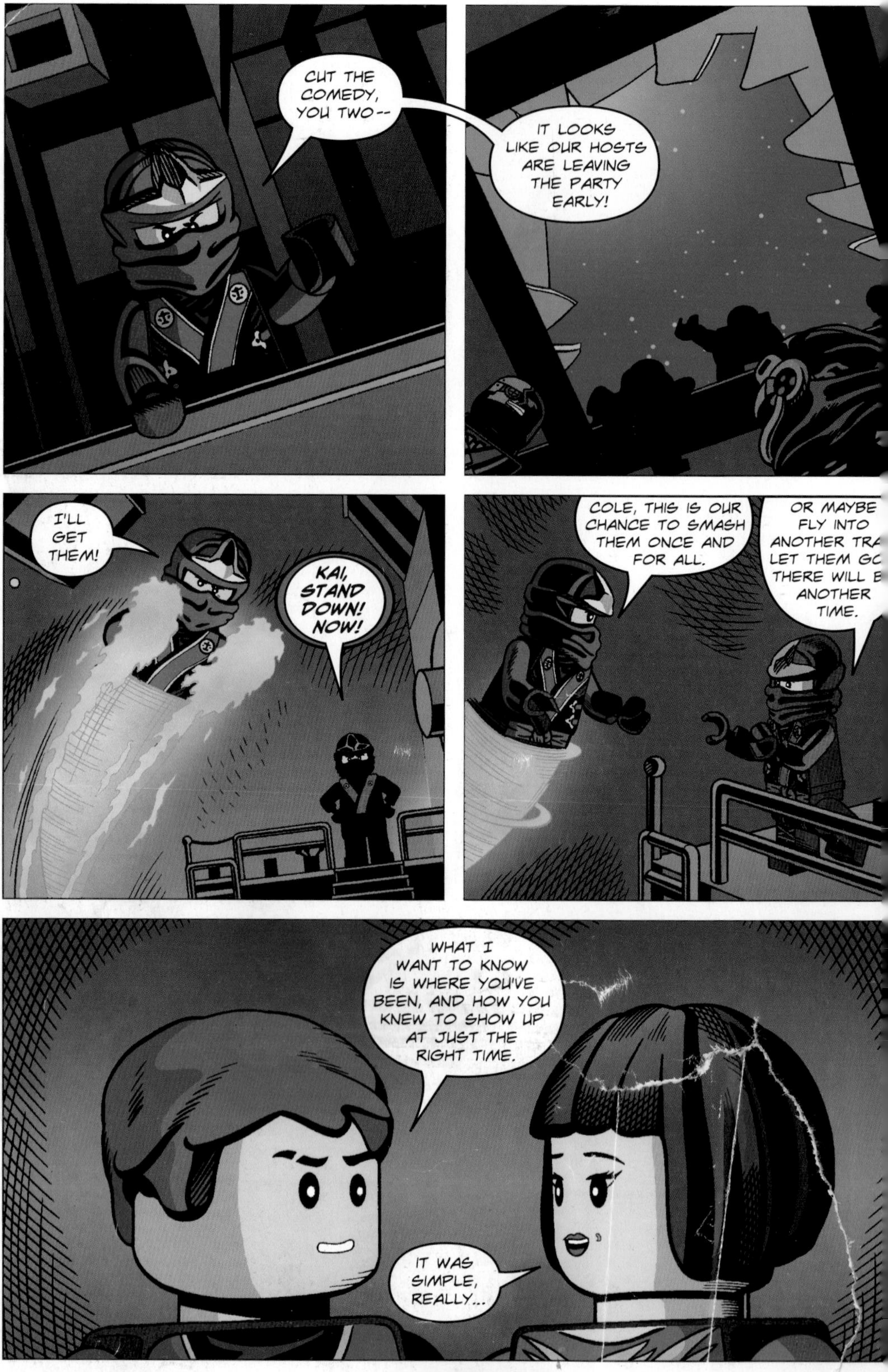
CUT THE COMEDY, YOU TWO--
IT LOOKS LIKE OUR HOSTS ARE LEAVING THE PARTY EARLY!
I'LL GET THEM!
KAI, STAND DOWN! NOW!
COLE, THIS IS OUR CHANCE TO SMASH THEM ONCE AND FOR ALL.
OR MAYBE FLY INTO ANOTHER TRA LET THEM GO THERE WILL B ANOTHER TIME.
WHAT I WANT TO KNOW IS WHERE YOU'VE BEEN, AND HOW YOU KNEW TO SHOW UP AT JUST THE RIGHT TIME.
IT WAS SIMPLE, REALLY...

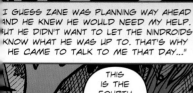

I GUESS ZANE WAS PLANNING WAY AHEAD AND HE KNEW HE WOULD NEED MY HELP. BUT HE DIDN'T WANT TO LET THE NINDROIDS KNOW WHAT HE WAS UP TO. THAT'S WHY HE CAME TO TALK TO ME THAT DAY..."

THIS IS THE FOURTH TIME I HAVE TOLD YOU THIS!

PLEASE TRY TO FOLLOW. IT'S IMPORTANT TO ME!

"AFTER HE LEFT, I WAS PUZZLED."

THE FOURTH TIME? HE NEVER SAID ANYTHING TO ME ABOUT ANY OF THIS BEFORE.

"THEN I REMEMBERED THE CODE HE AND I CREATED ONCE, IN CASE OF TROUBLE. IF A NUMBER IS IN THE SENTENCE, YOU USE THAT TO SPOT THE MESSAGE IN THE OTHER SENTENCES."

HE SAID "FOURTH," SO I SHOULD COUNT EVERY FOURTH WORD...

GOT IT! "FOLLOW ME... WAIT YOUR TIME... TELL NO ONE."

A WAS DOWING THROUGH L OUR TTLES," NG OUT NINDROID COULD WAITING SAVE E DAY.

YOU HAVEN'T WON ANYTHING! YOU--

OH, BE QUIET.

KZZZZAKK

57

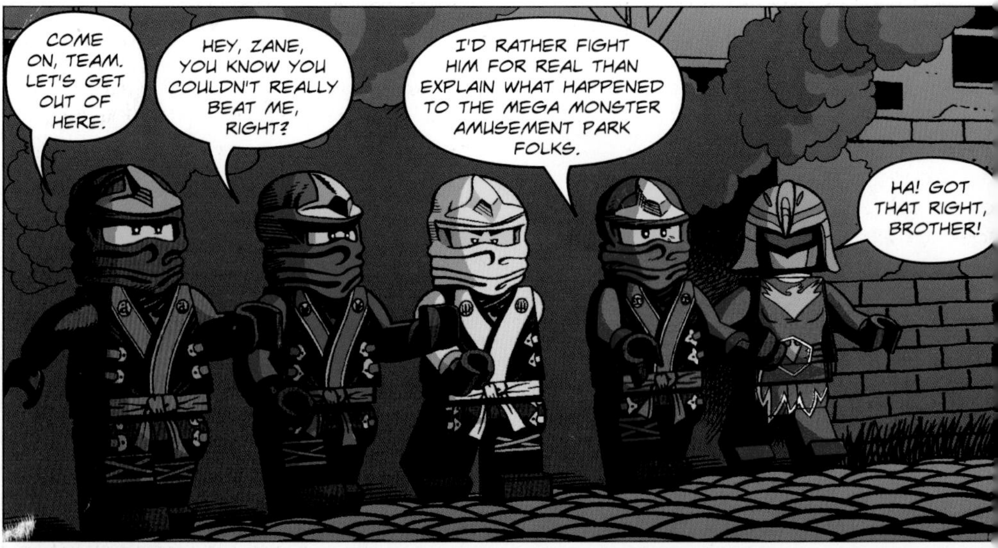
COME ON, TEAM. LET'S GET OUT OF HERE.
HEY, ZANE, YOU KNOW YOU COULDN'T REALLY BEAT ME, RIGHT?
I'D RATHER FIGHT HIM FOR REAL THAN EXPLAIN WHAT HAPPENED TO THE MEGA MONSTER AMUSEMENT PARK FOLKS.
HA! GOT THAT RIGHT, BROTHER!

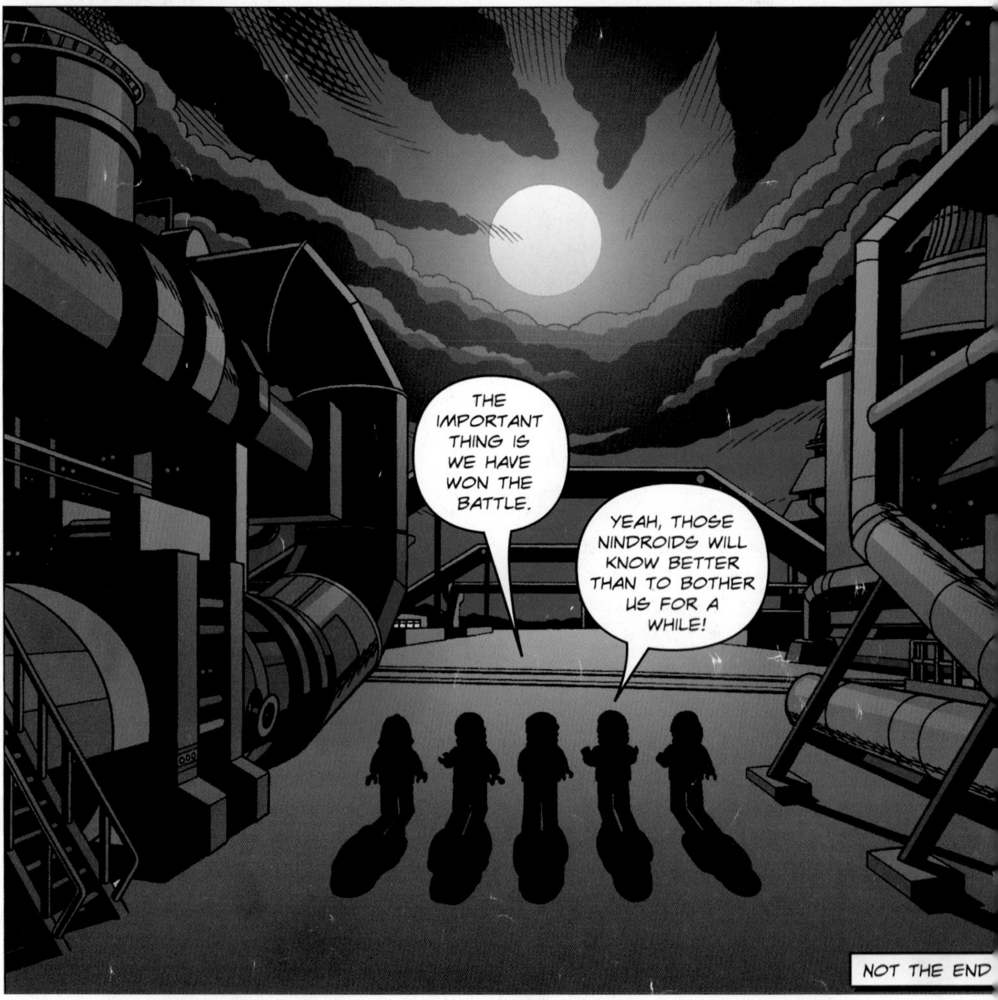
THE IMPORTANT THING IS WE HAVE WON THE BATTLE.
YEAH, THOSE NINDROIDS WILL KNOW BETTER THAN TO BOTHER US FOR A WHILE!
NOT THE END

WATCH OUT FOR PAPERCUTZ™

Welcome to the Nindroid-infested ninth LEGO® NINJAGO graphic novel by Greg Farshtey and Jolyon Yates from Papercutz, the constructible comics company dedicated to publishing great graphic novels for all ages. I'm Jim Salicrup, the ever-expanding Editor-in-Chief and first-in-line-at-the-upcoming THE LEGO MOVIE!

Not to get too preachy, but I do want to touch on one of the big themes in the previous two stories—and that's about belonging. While we may not be Nindroids, we humans are wired with a strong desire to belong, to be included, to be loved. Sometimes that desire is so strong inside us we may do things that aren't in our best interests. For example, many questionable organizations are very skilled at finding folks who are feeling alone and left out and turning them to "the Dark Side." It may sound like something out of a movie or comicbook, but it really does happen. These "cults" or whatever you want to call them, are usually organizations that exploit those feelings and trick hapless souls into joining their phony "families." It's a really scary thing, and I hope you are never forced to join any group like that.

That's not to say, by any stretch of the imagination, that all groups are bad. For example, there are groups that consist of people who just enjoy collecting LEGO or comics—and some who enjoy collecting comics about LEGO NINJAGO! It's great to have friends with similar interests—even if you don't agree with each other 100%. The point is, you're not alone. There are people out there who enjoy what you enjoy and "get it."

But one thing to keep in mind, is that everyone feels alone or apart sometimes. Don't forget that you're not the only one with feelings. Maybe we can all be a little nicer to our family, friends, and everyone else! Would it hurt to be kind to your teacher or boss or neighbor? Just smiling and saying hello to someone could be enough to cheer 'em up!

I've been involved in the world of comics a long time, and I've met many people who have had difficult childhoods, but because they enjoyed either comics or a particular TV show, they somehow managed to get through it! They knew that no matter how tough things were, Spider-Man or Papa Smurf or the Green Ninja would be there for them. Yes, they knew that these were all fictional characters, but when that's all you got—those characters can seem very real.

Well, enough of that! I just hope all of you know how much all of us at Papercutz appreciate you! After all, you help make our dreams come true by supporting such Papercutz graphic novels as LEGO NINJAGO! What? You didn't know that getting to produce comics every day, and work with some of the very best writers, artists, colorists, letterers, designers, and editors in the comicbook biz was my dream? Well, of course it was! And for your support, we can only say THANK YOU, don't miss LEGO NINJAGO #10 "The Phantom Ninja," and we wish all your dreams come true too!

Jim

STAY IN TOUCH!

EMAIL: salicrup@papercutz.com
WEB: papercutz.com
TWITTER: @papercutzgn
FACEBOOK: PAPERCUTZGRAPHICNOVELS
FAN MAIL: Papercutz, 160 Broadway, Suite 700, East Wing, New York, NY 10038

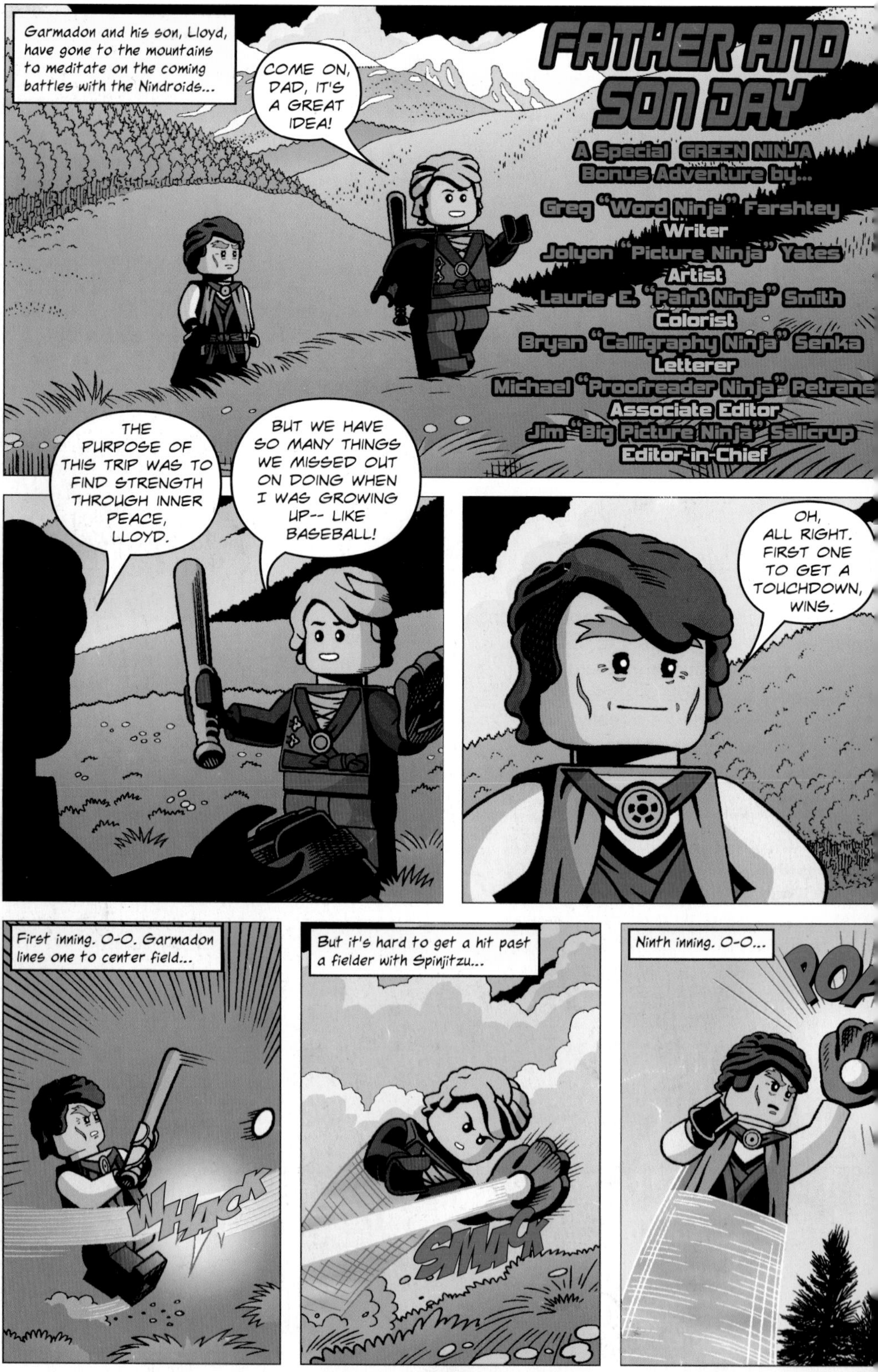
Garmadon and his son, Lloyd, have gone to the mountains to meditate on the coming battles with the Nindroids...
COME ON, DAD, IT'S A GREAT IDEA!
FATHER AND SON DAY
A Special GREEN NINJA Bonus Adventure by...
Greg "Word Ninja" Farshtey
Writer
Jolyon "Picture Ninja" Yates
Artist
Laurie E. "Paint Ninja" Smith
Colorist
Bryan "Calligraphy Ninja" Senka
Letterer
Michael "Proofreader Ninja" Petranek
Associate Editor
Jim "Big Picture Ninja" Salicrup
Editor-in-Chief
THE PURPOSE OF THIS TRIP WAS TO FIND STRENGTH THROUGH INNER PEACE, LLOYD.
BUT WE HAVE SO MANY THINGS WE MISSED OUT ON DOING WHEN I WAS GROWING UP-- LIKE BASEBALL!
OH, ALL RIGHT. FIRST ONE TO GET A TOUCHDOWN, WINS.
First inning. 0-0. Garmadon lines one to center field...
WHACK
But it's hard to get a hit past a fielder with Spinjitzu...
SMACK
Ninth inning. 0-0...
PO

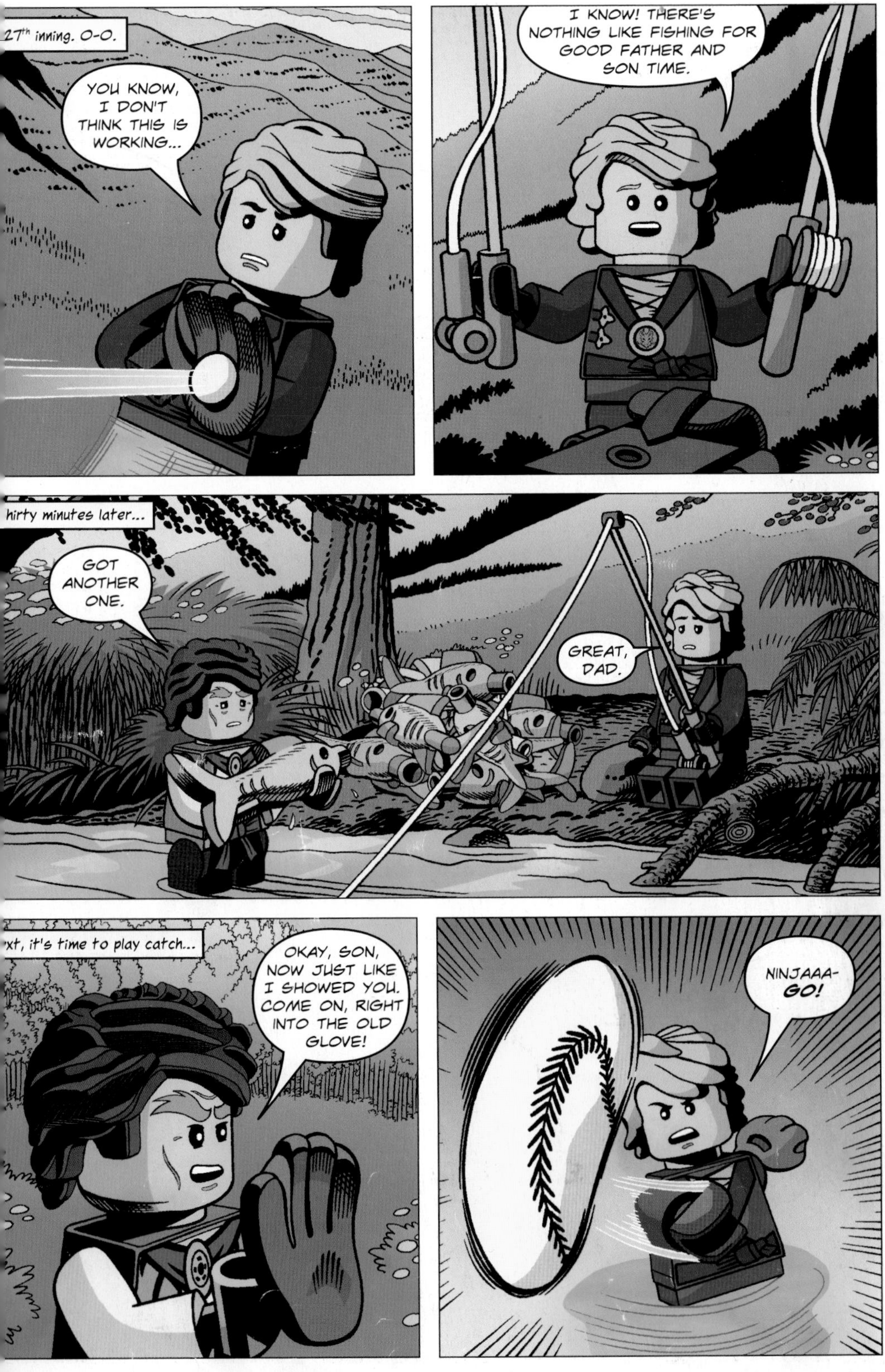
27th inning. 0-0.
YOU KNOW, I DON'T THINK THIS IS WORKING...
I KNOW! THERE'S NOTHING LIKE FISHING FOR GOOD FATHER AND SON TIME.
hirty minutes later...
GOT ANOTHER ONE.
GREAT, DAD.
xt, it's time to play catch...
OKAY, SON, NOW JUST LIKE I SHOWED YOU. COME ON, RIGHT INTO THE OLD GLOVE!
NINJAAA-GO!

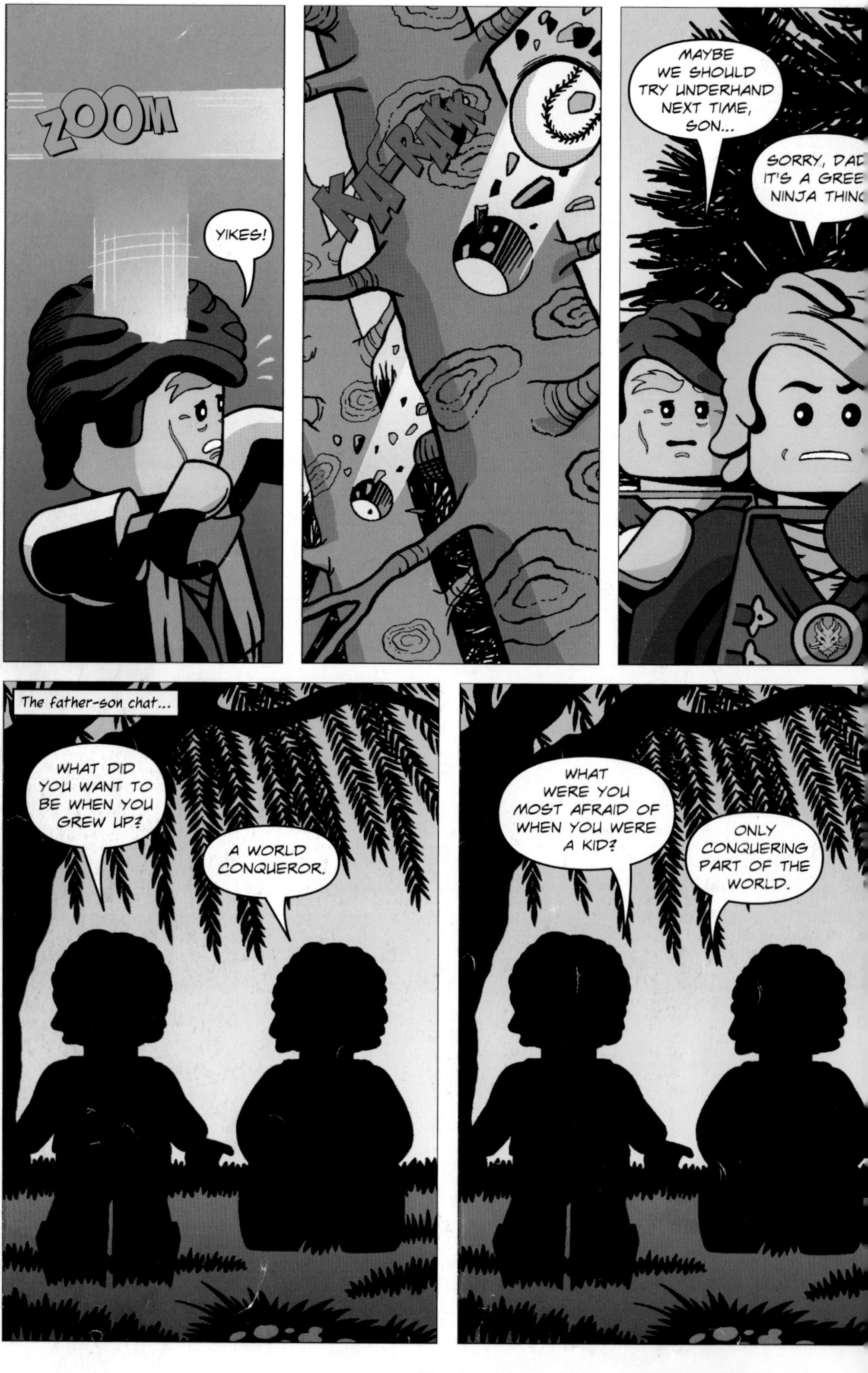
ZOOM
YIKES!
KA-RAK
MAYBE WE SHOULD TRY UNDERHAND NEXT TIME, SON...
SORRY, DAD IT'S A GREE NINJA THING
The father-son chat...
WHAT DID YOU WANT TO BE WHEN YOU GREW UP?
A WORLD CONQUEROR.
WHAT WERE YOU MOST AFRAID OF WHEN YOU WERE A KID?
ONLY CONQUERING PART OF THE WORLD.

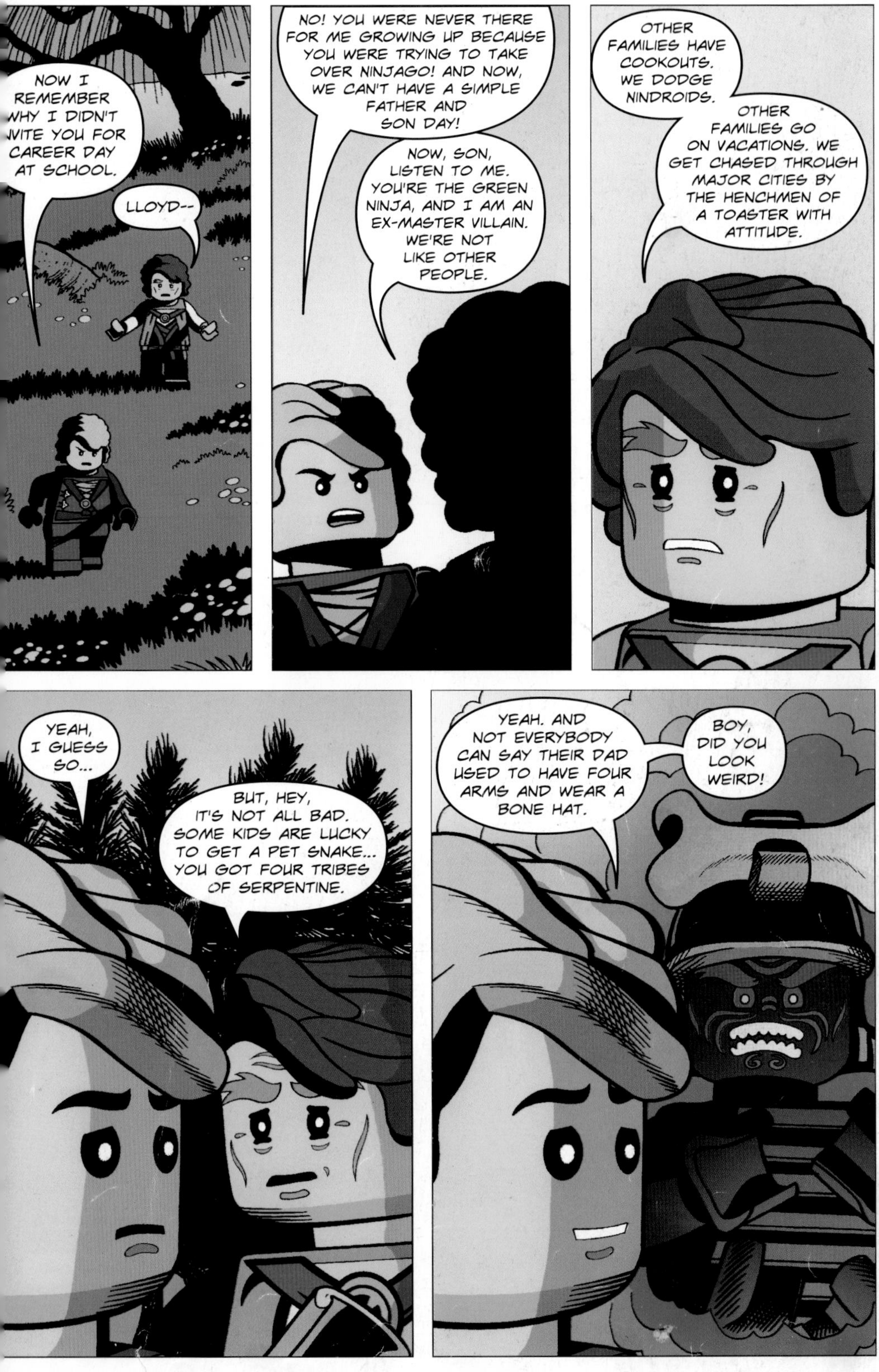
NOW I REMEMBER WHY I DIDN'T INVITE YOU FOR CAREER DAY AT SCHOOL.
LLOYD--
NO! YOU WERE NEVER THERE FOR ME GROWING UP BECAUSE YOU WERE TRYING TO TAKE OVER NINJAGO! AND NOW, WE CAN'T HAVE A SIMPLE FATHER AND SON DAY!
NOW, SON, LISTEN TO ME. YOU'RE THE GREEN NINJA, AND I AM AN EX-MASTER VILLAIN. WE'RE NOT LIKE OTHER PEOPLE.
OTHER FAMILIES HAVE COOKOUTS. WE DODGE NINDROIDS.
OTHER FAMILIES GO ON VACATIONS. WE GET CHASED THROUGH MAJOR CITIES BY THE HENCHMEN OF A TOASTER WITH ATTITUDE.
YEAH, I GUESS SO...
BUT, HEY, IT'S NOT ALL BAD. SOME KIDS ARE LUCKY TO GET A PET SNAKE... YOU GOT FOUR TRIBES OF SERPENTINE.
YEAH. AND NOT EVERYBODY CAN SAY THEIR DAD USED TO HAVE FOUR ARMS AND WEAR A BONE HAT.
BOY, DID YOU LOOK WEIRD!

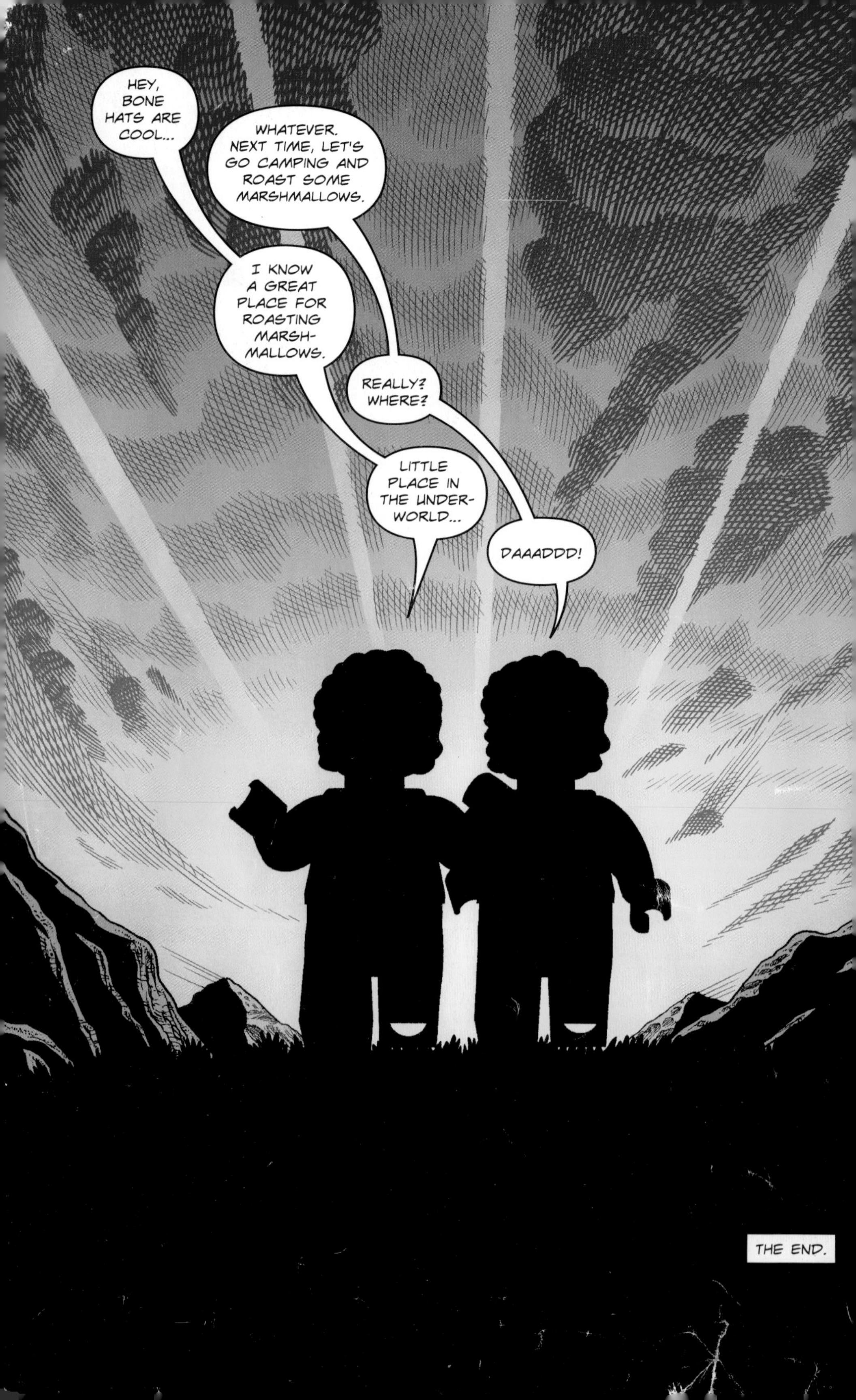
HEY, BONE HATS ARE COOL...
WHATEVER. NEXT TIME, LET'S GO CAMPING AND ROAST SOME MARSHMALLOWS.
I KNOW A GREAT PLACE FOR ROASTING MARSH-MALLOWS.
REALLY? WHERE?
LITTLE PLACE IN THE UNDER-WORLD...
DAAADDD!
THE END.